Miss Popularity
Goes Camping

candy apple books . . .
just for you.
sweet. fresh. fun.
take a bite!

Miss Popularity Goes Camping

FRANCESCO SEDITA

SCHOLASTIC INC.

New York Toronto London Auckland Sydney
Mexico City New Delhi Hong Kong Buenos Aires

No part of this publication may be reproduced, stored in a retrieval system, or transmitted in any form or by any means, electronic, mechanical, photocopying, recording, or otherwise, without written permission of the publisher. For information regarding permission, write to Scholastic Inc., Attention: Permissions Department, 557 Broadway, New York, NY 10012.

ISBN-13: 978-0-545-13215-2
ISBN-10: 0-545-13215-0

Text design by Steve Scott
The text type was set in Bulmer

12 11 10 9 8 7 6 5 4 3 2 1   9 10 11 12 13 14 / 0
Printed in the U.S.A.
First printing, May 2009

To Craig, for always guiding the way.
And to Sean.

CHAPTER 1

Teal Crisis

Cassie Cyan Knight stood in front of her mirror, turning and spinning in her favorite pair of teal capris and a classic white button-down. But something was very wrong. The pants seemed so blah. So boring. So humdrum. *How could this be?* Cassie wondered. Teal was the best color in the galaxy.

Or was it?

She walked to her stereo, grabbed her teal iPod nano, and clicked to the playlist that her BTF (Best Texas Friend), Erin, had made for her. Track 1 swept out through the speakers, coating her chocolate-and-cream room with musical goodness. Cassie's spirits rose.

As she walked back to her mirror, Cassie looked at all the pictures she'd stuck on its frame. She and

1

her parents had moved to Maine only four months ago but already it was feeling like home. And Cassie was grateful. Sure, she missed her old life back in Houston, Texas — especially Erin and all of her other friends there — but now that she'd settled in to her new house and at Oak Grove, her new school, she was truly enjoying herself.

Cassie smiled as she scanned the pictures. Her favorite was the one of her and Etoile, her BMF (Best Maine Friend) taking their bows at the Oak Grove charity fashion show extravaganza they'd thrown the month before. Cassie still couldn't believe that she was lucky enough to find a friend like Etoile, the only other person at her musty new middle school who shared Cassie's passion for fashion.

Cassie glanced at the picture that was right beneath the one of her and Etoile. This one showed Cassie, Etoile, Jonah — Etoile's BGF (Best Guy Friend) since they were babies — and mean Mary Ellen McGinty. Cassie did her best to keep from automatically adding "mean" in front of "Mary Ellen" but she couldn't help it! Mary Ellen had been rude to Cassie since Cassie's beaded flat first stepped foot in Oak Grove's hallways. She'd even had the nerve to be mad that Cassie's fashion show idea was chosen over her own tree-planting idea for the school's charity event. Though Mary Ellen had eventually come to accept Cassie's idea, there was still a tension between the two girls.

Just then, the new Beyoncé song zoomed out of the speakers. Cassie swayed her hips, closed her eyes, and imagined herself walking down a big crystal staircase, on her world tour. She was going to open her eyes and — voilà! — teal pants would rule once again. At the count of three:

One, two —

Please, please, please!

"Cassie!"

Her mother's voice startled her and she whipped around, her red curls catching in her LuLu Island lip gloss.

"Oh, hi!" she said, half laughing, half totally embarrassed.

"Honey, Etoile is on the phone for you." Cassie's mom handed the phone to Cassie. "And what did I tell you about the music? Let's keep it at 'six' or below on the dial, okay, superstar?" She lowered the volume, smiling.

Cassie took the phone. "Okay, sorry. I know it was loud, it's just, well, I was having a fashion emergency!"

Her mom walked out of Cassie's room, shaking her head.

"You're not going to believe this," Cassie said into the phone.

"Oh no, what?" Etoile asked back, her voice steady, clearly ready for a crisis.

"I don't think I like my teal pants anymore!"

"What? The capris with the little drawstrings?"

"Yes, those ones!"

"Cass, you loved them this weekend. You even told me you were excited to debut them this week, in honor of spring. I mean, you planned the actual day to reveal them!"

"I know. I know! It's supposed to be tomorrow!" Cassie examined herself in the mirror. "There's just something not right," Cassie said sadly. "I know this is going to sound crazy, but I don't know if I . . . love the color." It pained Cassie to say it.

Now Etoile was worried. "But, teal is your . . ."

"Signature color." Cassie sighed. She slumped down onto her bed. What was going on?

"Relax!" Etoile said. "Just take a deep breath and don't think about it. It's some weird lighting thing, I bet."

Cassie sighed. "You're right." She looked out the window and sighed again. Only two sighs are ever allowed at once, otherwise it's just drama for the sake of drama. "So what's up?" she asked, feeling slightly calmer.

"I was going through some of the Fash Bash pics on my laptop just now for Yearbook, and I found the cutest one of us backstage! We have to — *have to!* — get it in Yearbook."

Cassie and Etoile had just joined Yearbook together as photo editors. It was so fun to go through all the pictures and help decide which ones were the best.

"I can't wait to see it!" Cassie said. She stood up then and looked out the window. The May sunlight was a bright, yummy yellow, but there was still some snow on the ground! But the girls in Texas had told Cassie their hair was already frizzing from the humidity.

Yay, Maine! Cassie thought, happy that her red curls were still frizz-free. She smiled then, overcome with excitement for her first summer in Maine and all the new things she'd be doing. Erin was even planning to visit from Texas, and Cassie couldn't wait to give her friend a tour of their beautiful mall, introduce her to the sheer deliciousness of Maine's blueberries, and show her the high school of performing arts.

Cassie loved driving past it. She *so* wanted to go there!

"You know, we have a lot more work to do for Yearbook," Etoile said.

"I know!" Cassie plunked down on her bed and opened her teal planner. She and Etoile had made a list of all of the pics they wanted to submit. They still had the entire year of sports to research, and they were both dreading it. Sports were cool for people who liked them, but they were too confusing for Cassie.

"We have to start Sports soon, you know," Cassie said.

"Right," Etoile said, clearly as disappointed as Cassie.

There was a knock at Cassie's door. Her mom popped her head in. "Honey, your dad's home. Let's have some dinner."

"Okay, Sheila," Cassie said, realizing she was hungry. She knew she was a rarity among her friends, to call her parents by their first names. "Mom" and "Dad" just felt so Disney Channel sometimes.

"E, I have to run to dinner."

"Oh, wait! Before you go, did you hear that the sixth grade is having a special assembly tomorrow?" Etoile asked.

6

"We are?" Cassie gasped, intrigued. "What about?"

"I bet it's about the spring class trip!" Etoile replied.

Cassie loved class trips. In Houston, they always went on a fall trip and a spring one. And Cassie loved them all. One time they went to NASA and got to try on space suits and even got to sit in a flight simulator. Erin had just told Cassie that this year they were going to Six Flags Over Texas.

"I'm not sure. But I have to go to dinner now, too, I'm starving."

"I don't know why you didn't just finish your lunch today," Cassie said incredulously.

"That chicken was SO gross!" Etoile squealed.

"It was not. It was delicious."

"I swear it was still clucking!" Etoile said, laughing.

"I think you're still clucking," Cassie said.

"Cluck! Cluck!"

"Talk to you later, chickie!"

"Love you," Etoile said.

"Loves!"

Cassie clicked off the phone and ran to dinner. She hoped they weren't having chicken.

CHAPTER 2

Up for an Adventure?

The next day at school, Cassie was dressed in her teal best. She'd decided that the only way to rediscover teal was to celebrate it. And she did so by wearing her teal capris and a sweet "Little Miss Giggles" pink tee from Kitson. She had seen a pic of the adorable Emma Watson in a magazine, shopping at Kitson in Los Angeles. If the shop was good for smarty-pants Hermoine, it was certainly good enough for Cassie!

She stood at her locker, her feet chilly in her cute peekaboo sandals. Even though it was still pretty cold outside, it was officially springtime, and Cassie was ready for some sandal love.

Her cell phone beeped and she dug through her purse to find it.

JST SYNG HI! HI!

It was Erin.

Cassie typed back, quickly, imagining Erin running through the thick Texas air to catch the school bus.

HI! OFFICIALLY IN SANDALS! YAY! XO

She hit SEND and turned off her phone. No phones in school for Cassie. She just didn't get it. She loaded up her bag with the books she needed for morning classes. As she spun the dial on her lock, Etoile came around the corner, looking simply divine, as always. Today, she had on a pleated skirt that gave Cassie serious skirt envy. A perfect, flouncy tennis skirt. Bright green. Superchic.

"What's up, *Project Runway*?" Cassie called to Etoile. Of course, as always, Etoile blushed.

"Do you really like it?"

"I LA-HOVE it."

"Thanks! It's a total thrift store buy," Etoile said, piling a ton of books into her locker. "Pre-al quiz today, right?" she asked.

"Don't remind me!" Cassie groaned. Cassie and pre-al were *not* getting along these days.

9

"You'll do fine," Etoile said. "You always do!"

The first bell rang.

"You are SO saved by the bell right now," Cassie said to Etoile, a smile curling her lips.

The two girls walked together to morning assembly.

The sixth grade class gathered in the auditorium. Cassie and Etoile walked over to where Jonah and Seth Gordon were sitting. Seth had transferred to Oak Grove from Pottsville Prep a year ago, and he and Jonah had become really good friends, just like Cassie and Etoile.

"Mornin'!" Cassie said as she sat down.

Etoile didn't speak. Because she and Jonah had grown up together, they sometimes treated each other like brother and sister.

"Hi, Etoile," Seth said.

Etoile barely looked up from her backpack, which she was digging through. "Hey," she said awkwardly.

Cassie looked at her in disbelief. What was up with Etoile?

"So, we're going on a class trip?" Cassie asked.

"I don't know," Jonah said. "I hope so."

"Me, too!" Cassie exclaimed so loudly that Lynn Bauman, one of Mary Ellen's best friends, turned

her head to see what was going on. Their e[y]
met and they both laughed. Mary Ellen turned and
did her best to smile, too, but it looked more like
a scowl.

Cassie didn't care. She was too excited for the
assembly to start.

"Dude," Jonah whispered to Cassie. "I can't
believe Mary Ellen still totally hates you because
you did the fashion show."

Cassie punched Jonah in the arm. "She does not
hate me! There is no hate here!"

Jonah laughed.

Cassie was about to punch him again but
Principal Veronica walked onto the stage and
directly over to the microphone. She was wearing
her boring old gray suit, gray shoes, and a bun
piled high on her head.

"When is she going to wear something different?" Cassie whispered to Etoile. They both loved
PV — that was what they called her — but she
needed some color in her wardrobe!

"Oak Grovians!" PV said, pride bursting
from her every cell. She started every announce-
ment that way: confident, cheery, proud. Maybe
Cassie would get sick of it someday, but it
still gave her chills every time. PV was really
amazing.

is a very special day, when we announce __ grade class trip, a rite of passage for every at Oak Grove."

sie's heart soared. It *was* a class trip. Hooray! Maybe they would go to a lake retreat house? Or maybe even a visit to a neighboring state?

"This year, we are thrilled to be sending you to The Gamut."

Cassie looked at Etoile and raised her eyebrows. She didn't know what The Gamut was, but she heard a few murmurs from people around her. They sounded like happy murmurs, which gave her some confidence that it was going to be a trip that she liked.

"As many of you know, The Gamut is one of the best camping experiences any young person growing up in Maine can have," PV said.

Cassie's heart skipped three beats. *"Camping?"* she whispered to Etoile. What kind of class trip was that?

Etoile shrugged her shoulders.

"Camping is a vital aspect to a well-rounded learning experience," PV continued. "We cannot limit our quest for knowledge to books or, simply, to the indoors. Instead, we must turn our gazes outside of the classroom and come to appreciate and understand the beauty of the world around us.

Yours will be the first Oak Grove class to attend The Gamut and I am certain that this trip will not only educate you, but challenge you — and help you to push yourselves to great excellence."

Cassie's mind instantly flooded with images of creepy-crawlies, outhouses, and things that went bump in the night. Then she took a deep breath. She'd never been camping before and really didn't know if it would be as bad as she imagined. And Cassie certainly wasn't someone who was afraid to try new things.

PV continued, "Your homeroom teachers will tell you more, so please continue to your assigned classrooms. You are dismissed. Best of luck to you!"

By the time the speech was over, Cassie was bursting with excitement and positive energy. This trip might turn out to be a lot of fun. Maybe even life-changing!

Cassie and her fellow students gathered up their things and headed to their homerooms.

"Don't be nervous about this," Etoile told Cassie, as they said good-bye to each other for the morning.

"Nervous? What's there to be nervous about?" Cassie asked calmly.

Surprise flashed across Etoile's face. "Oh, nothing! Really! I just didn't know if you'd been camping before."

"Nope. I haven't. And I can't wait!" Cassie said, beaming.

Cassie walked into Mr. Blackwell's homeroom. Of course, as soon as she turned the corner into the classroom — her favorite one at Oak Grove, because it was warm and cozy with a fireplace and dark wood desks — she saw Mary Ellen, sitting there, talking to Lynn and their BFF, Deirdre. Mary Ellen seemed really excited and kept pointing to a brightly colored brochure that was spread out on her desk.

Cassie smiled politely in their direction and hurried to her desk. She took out her brand-new tiara marabou pen and matching pink notebook and began reviewing her pre-algebra homework, hoping it would help for the quiz.

Life Rule # 41: It's okay if something doesn't come easily. It is super-duper NOT okay to ignore it.

Just as she was making sure a + b actually did = c, Mr. Blackwell spoke.

14

"Good morning everyone. Let's get settled," he said. "As you've just heard, we have some big news for you today."

The classroom quieted down, and everyone gave their attention to Mr. B. That was the best thing about Mr. B's classroom: He treated all of his students with respect. And everyone respected him back. Like when the entire class messed up on a pop quiz after a nightly reading assignment. That was a big one. But, *hello*, it was the *American Idol* finale the night before! Sometimes television is very *very* important! Of course, Mr. B was totally cool about it and gave them another chance. He even admitted that he watched the finale, too, which made his coolness factor skyrocket!

He put his glasses up on his head and they disappeared into his curly black hair. "I thought I would pass out some information on The Gamut," he said. Mr. B picked up a stack of brochures from his desk. They looked like the one Mary Ellen had. As people passed the brochures around, Mr. Blackwell read aloud.

"The Gamut is a one-of-a-kind adventure camp where students will see Maine in a brand-new way. Not only will time be spent learning about the natural habitat of our state, participants will also be able to experience it all. Hiking and rock climbing on natural cliffs, rafting trips, and camping out are just some of the ways students will be able to enjoy themselves while learning about Maine's rich natural beauty."

Natural beauty sounded great to Cassie! As soon as the brochure was passed to her, she unfolded it eagerly. There were photos of gorgeous sunsets and forests and campfires. People were even cooking hot dogs! It looked fabulous.

But Cassie's heart dropped when she flipped to the back panel. There, she saw people bungee jumping, canoeing, and even pitching tents. Cassie's pulse was racing suddenly. Some of those activities looked kind of scary.

"We are thrilled to have you guys be Oak Grove's first class to visit The Gamut. A special thanks to Mary Ellen and her mom for all of their help in setting this up." Mr. B smiled at Mary Ellen, and she grinned with sheer pride.

Mary Ellen and *her mom? Uh-oh,* Cassie thought.

Mary Ellen turned from her seat in the front row to look at the class. Her eyes met Cassie's for a moment.

Sure, things had been okay between the two girls since the Fash Bash. They said hello, and Mary Ellen even turned her frown into a smile sometimes. But still, Cassie wasn't sure that they were ready for a trip into the wilderness together.

Mr. Blackwell then passed around a list of items they needed for the trip.

🌿 THE OAK GROVE SCHOOL 🌿

What to Bring on Your Camping Trip

The most important thing to remember when packing for a trip to The Gamut is "Plan for the worst and hope for the best."

Here are the items we suggest each student bring:

Clothing
2 pants
2 shirts
1 pair of hiking boots
1 belt
1 medium-weight jacket
Sleep clothes
Undergarments
Socks
1 warm hat
1 pair of gloves

Toiletries
Toothbrush, toothpaste
Soap, shampoo
Comb, brush
Washcloth, towel

Miscellaneous
Insect repellent
Sunglasses
Sunscreen, lip balm
1 sleeping bag
1 pillow

Cassie's eyes scanned the list. She couldn't believe how limited it was. It said "lip balm" but what about gloss? And only two pairs of pants? How was she supposed to make it through this teal crisis if she didn't bring at least three different color options?

She took a deep breath, folded the list neatly, and put it in her backpack. Just as she zippered it up, she looked up and saw Mary Ellen staring at her with a sugary smile on her face.

Cassie wasn't sure if she was imagining things, but she could have sworn Mary Ellen mouthed the words *Good luck*. Cassie's stomach filled with butterflies.

"Guys, there's also a permission slip here for your parents. Please get that back to us by Friday," Mr. Blackwell said, passing out the slips. "This is going to be a real adventure for all of us," he said enthusiastically. "I can't wait!"

"Me neither!" Mary Ellen shouted back, flipping her hair.

Life Rule #44: You don't flip your hair in a scrunchy.
(And, oh yeah, Life Rule #43: You don't wear scrunchies!)

At lunch, Cassie waited until she and Etoile were alone at their Freak-Out Table before she admitted to being nervous about the trip.

Cassie and Etoile always sat at one of two tables. One was private, the Freak-Out Table — reserved for freak-outs, naturally, and alone time, so the two girls could talk in private. The other was in the center of the cafeteria, called the Be Seen Table — and that was for all other times.

"Okay, you were right before," Cassie said. "Maybe I am a little worried about camping."

"Did you see the brochure in homeroom?" Etoile asked.

"Yeah," Cassie said, sipping her water.

"You have to admit, it looks really beautiful," Etoile said.

"But did you see the activities?" Cassie asked.

"Totally scary."

"I know!" Cassie squealed.

"Oh, so what? It's going to be great!"

Cassie was quiet for a moment.

"What's the matter, Cass?" Etoile asked.

"I have to be honest, I'm nervous about Mary Ellen *and* her mom coming on the trip. . . ." Cassie said.

Etoile, the ever-understanding friend, nodded. "I know. I wondered how you'd feel."

"It just worries me," Cassie said, thinking.

"That's why we're at the Freak-Out Table," Etoile said, laughing.

Cassie smiled.

"You guys have been okay, right? It seems like it, anyway," Etoile continued.

Cassie sighed. "This could be the end of me," she said dramatically. She bit into her veggie sandwich.

"Oh, come on! It is so not the end of *anyone*," Etoile said, playfully throwing a chip at Cassie. "We are going to do it together, and we're going to have fun!"

"Really?" Cassie asked tentatively. She took a deep breath.

"Really!" Etoile beamed, all starry and light. Then she reached into her backpack and pulled out a copy of *Teen Vogue*. "P.S., I've been wanting to show you this since this morning. Check it out!" Etoile opened the magazine to a dog-eared page and held it up. It was Miley Cyrus in a fab frock. The dress — a *gorgeous thing*, or GT, as they called it — was gray, with ruffles for days, with a darling little black bolero over it.

"Oh my, GT!" Cassie squealed, and pulled the magazine out of Etoile's hands.

"I was thinking that maybe I could try to make something like that," Etoile said in a little bit of a whisper. Etoile often got shy and lowered her voice when she spoke about her designs.

"You have to! You would make it even cuter than this one, I just know it," Cassie said, her heart thumping in her chest. She was always wowed by Etoile's talent.

Cassie flipped through the rest of Etoile's favorite fashions in the magazine, stopping at each of her dog-eared pages. A fashion tidal wave washed over her and she started to feel hopeful.

"Do you think," Cassie asked sheepishly, "we could bring magazines on the camping trip?"

"Of course! And we can stay up late with flash-lights and stuff and read!" Etoile responded giddily.

Cassie's smile got even wider. "That would be so great."

"How is the teal crisis going?" Etoile asked sympathetically.

Cassie looked down at her capris, which were really adorable even in the bad caf lighting. "I think we're okay right now. Not totally sure."

"But better than last night?" Etoile asked.

"Yes," Cassie said happily.

Just then, Mary Ellen walked by their table, her hair twisted and tangled even tighter into her ratty old scrunchy. Cassie wondered why the girl insisted on doing that to her potentially pretty hair.

"Hey, Mary Ellen," Etoile said.

"Hi, guys," Mary Ellen said, her voice perkier than usual. She stopped for a moment and Cassie cringed. Was she going to sit with them? Cassie *was not* ready for that. Not even a little bit!

"I just want you to know," Mary Ellen continued, "that I am so excited about The Gamut."

"We are, too," Cassie said, trying desperately to sound like she meant it.

"You are? That's so good to hear. We were all worried about you," Mary Ellen said, smiling.

"Nope, she's fine!" Etoile said.

"Well, good. Because it's going to be really special! I even get to plan the final night's party. And it's going to be really fun," Mary Ellen said. She looked at Cassie and cocked her head. "It's not going to be a fashion show, though. Sorry!" She smiled again.

"That's not a problem," Etoile said coolly.

"Oh, and, Cassie," Mary Ellen said, sugar-voiced, "I don't think you can bring all of those magazines on the trip. Just so you know. They'll be too heavy for the hike to the site." She beamed. Cassie wanted to believe Mary Ellen was just being nice and watching out for her. She really did.

But, c'mon, people!

"Um, thanks?" Cassie said, unsure.

"Sure! If you have any questions about what to bring — or wear — feel free to ask me, okay? This *definitely* isn't about fashion, so you're really going to have to be smart about it all." And then, Mary Ellen flipped her hair and walked away.

"Hmm," Etoile said curiously, "does Mary Ellen think that she's being nice when she talks like that?"

"I don't think so," Cassie said, feeling down. "I *think* she just told me I wasn't smart."

Etoile and Cassie both looked at each other sadly. Cassie put the magazine down. She suddenly wasn't in the mood for frocks.

That night, Cassie logged on for her nightly IM with Erin. She sat at her computer right at eight P.M., still mulling over a pesky math problem from her homework assignment. There was so much on her mind, and pre-al seemed to be the only thing that could distract her.

When she opened her IM, Erin was already there, waiting.

Life Rule 59: Love and friendship can survive very long distances.

4EVRRN: Donny McMahill was elected class president for next year!
MISSCASS: Wow! That is SO great! He's perfect for the job.
4EVRRN: O PLZ! Would have totally been u if u were still here in TX! Everyone still misses u!
MISSCASS: UR sweet.
MISSCASS: Our class trip just got announced.
4EVRRN: And??
MISSCASS: Camping.
4EVRRN: Oh . . . ☹

Cassie imagined the Houston trip to Six Flags. Screaming on roller coasters, eating too much pink cotton candy, and laughing the whole way through.

MISSCASS: It gets worse. . . .
4EVRRN: It's a trip to find Bigfoot? ☺

Cassie laughed.

MISSCASS: Mary Ellen is peer leader. And her mom is coming!!

Cassie waited for the little icon to blink. Erin must have been writing an entire book of advice, understanding, and total sympathy.

But nothing happened. No blinking. No words. Not even a "BRB!"

She waited another moment, and still, nothing. Cassie couldn't take it any longer so she typed back furiously.

MISSCASS: Umm, hello??!

Then there was blinking from the other end. Erin was typing. Finally!

4EVRRN: Wear these.

Just then, a pic of the cutest boots popped up.

4EVRRN: How could camping be bad if you can wear boots like this?! Sending you the <u>link</u>. And look at the name!

Cassie dutifully clicked the link, and she saw the boots — and the name. RedHead! There was a company named RedHead that actually made camping gear. Was this a sign?

MISSCASS: WOW!!
4EVRRN: How cool are those?
MISSCASS: And the name?!!
4EVRRN: I know! See, it's a sign or something. It's going to be okay.
MISSCASS: OK. UR right. Thanks. Gonna buy them right now.
4EVRRN: Luv 4EVS!
MISSCASS: Totes. xo

Cassie logged off and clicked onto the Web site. The boots were super cute. Pinkish and mossy swirls. Real soles so hiking would be okay in them, and calf-high, so no water worries. Chic and practical. Awesome. Cassie sprang out of her chair and ran downstairs to ask her mom to order them.

As her red locks bounced behind her, Cassie took a deep breath. Someone had to reinvent camp wear, and she and Etoile were the two girls to do it!

CHAPTER 3

Can You Hike in Marabou?

It was time to get serious. Cassie only had two weeks to get herself ready for the trip to The Gamut. Since there was no time to write to Tim Gunn and the *Project Runway* judges for help, Cassie had done extensive online research and was ready to hit the mall. She and Etoile met on a bright, warm Saturday afternoon. Spring in Maine was proving to be really different than spring in Texas — cooler and crisper. Being so close to the ocean still amazed Cassie. She loved the smell of the salty water and feeling the breeze on her skin.

The two girls met at the mall at exactly one o'clock.

"Okay," Etoile said. "This is serious. We have exactly two hours to figure out what we *want*, what we *need*, and what we just *have to have* for this trip."

Cassie shook her head and straightened her thin headband. She was sure it was going to explode while holding back all her curls, but she loved it — a perfectly shiny green ribbon that shimmered in her hair. She had only admitted to Etoile that she'd gotten the idea from Mary Ellen, who wore headbands every now and then. Even the plainest ones were a million times better than those dreadful scrunchies.

Cassie grabbed Etoile's arm and they made an about-face. They pushed through the gleaming glass doors, a moment that always took Cassie's breath away. She loved the idea that so many different expressions of fashion fantasticness could exist under one roof.

"Let's do this," Cassie said.

They marched straight to Patagonia. There was a backpack that Cassie had seen online that she loved. They had it in teal but since she was in the midst of her teal crisis, she wasn't sure if she could commit. So, as a compromise, Etoile opted for the teal and Cassie bought green for herself. Cassie also picked up a cute little silver bag. She knew she should have gone for something maybe slightly more practical, but who could resist silver?

They left Patagonia with their bags, plenty of warm socks, lightweight gloves for nighttime, and some insect repellent that smelled like lemons. But now, Cassie and Etoile were at their most frightening frontier: jeans. Cassie wanted to head directly to the designer jeans, but Etoile stopped her in her tracks.

"No. No Sevens for camping," Etoile said seriously.

"But why not?"

"Because you're going *camping*, Cass. Let's be real here."

Cassie frowned.

Etoile knew there was only one way to cheer her up. Her Tim Gunn impersonation: "Cassie, I'm concerned that you're not really thinking this through. Your jeans should be a little less designer and a little more practical for camping, all right?"

Cassie laughed. "All right. Let's make it work, people!"

Giggling, Etoile grabbed Cassie's hand and led her to the Levi's section. Cassie knew this was why she and Etoile were fabulous shopping buddies. Cassie was all instinct. But Etoile? She was total and complete science. She knew how to find the best of the best no matter where they were. She pulled three different pairs from the shelves.

Cassie followed Etoile to the dressing rooms, and was soon behind the curtain, trying on the jeans, bopping her head to silly instrumental music. Cassie couldn't believe it: Each pair fit perfectly.

As she turned and twirled in front of the three-way mirror, Cassie fluffed up her hair, and pulled on her new backpack, to see how her signature camping look was coming together. So far, so good.

Elated, they ran from the dressing room with only a few minutes to spare before they met up with their moms for Cold Stone.

Cassie practically had to keep her eyes on the floor as they hurried through the cosmetics section. There was nothing like some good gloss or a shimmery shadow to make Cassie happy. She tried her best but couldn't resist. She looked up and saw the shiny, clean counters of colors, and her heart started to beat quickly.

Etoile caught on right away. "Cass, we don't have time for lip gloss!"

"There is always time for lip gloss!" And with that, she ran to the counter in front of them. Etoile followed.

Cassie saw it immediately. She couldn't believe her luck and timing. There, in front of her, was a lip gloss display. And the featured color?

Honeypot!

"E! Look at this!"

Etoile was preoccupied by another display but looked up, as Cassie held the adorable little tub of gloss out toward her.

Etoile read the label.

"Wait. Honeypot? Really?" Etoile asked.

"I know. It is perfect and adorable for a camping trip! I have to get it. It will complete my signature camping look."

"Absolutely!" Etoile said, approvingly.

As she tried the gloss on in the mirror, Cassie couldn't believe it. She and Etoile actually had created a chic signature camping look in less than two hours. Right down to the lip gloss.

Not even creepy-crawlies and bungee jumping could stop them now.

CHAPTER 4
Ready or Not!

It was finally here: The day when Cassie would gulp down her fears and worries, and get on the bus headed for The Gamut. That morning, she woke up, half nervous and half excited. New adventures were always something to look forward to, and this one was going to be a challenge. Sure, moving to Maine from Texas had been no small feat — but she had survived. Could camping be much harder?

She took her time getting ready that morning. It would be a while before she could shower in her own house again!

She began with her delicious Red Expressions Enhancing Shampoo — two cycles through her red locks, letting the foam bubble up and up. Once she'd rinsed that clean, she finished off with a big glob of fortifying treatment. Her poor hair was going to need all the help it could get out there in the woods! And even though it wasn't on the school list, Cassie decided she would smuggle in her Strengthening Spray. She could not be expected to let the wilderness devour her hair . . . the way a bear might devour the campsite.

Try as she might, Cassie wasn't able to keep those thoughts from creeping into her head sometimes. But she did her best to push this one away as she wrapped her hair in a towel.

She walked into her room and felt a pang of homesickness. This was the first time she was going to be away from their house in Maine. Cassie had spent the night at Etoile's many times but *this* was three whole days. Cassie couldn't believe how quickly she'd become attached to her new house. She felt like she was just beginning to get over missing Texas — and now she was already missing Maine!

Cassie put on a short-sleeved printed shirt in teal from the SJP BITTEN line — totally adorable. If this shirt didn't help to solve the teal crisis once and for all, nothing would! It had three adorable buttons at the neck and the sweetest little flower print. Subdued and sassy. And, to make the look super complete she added her newly purchased, comfy Levi's that were just so cute. It was the perfect outfit for the trip to The Gamut. She even decided to wear her new hiking boots on the bus. Cassie and her mom couldn't believe how well they fit when they arrived in the mail.

She grabbed her bags and clomped down the stairs to have breakfast with Sheila and Paul before she headed to the school. It was kind of cool that they were going to miss three days of classes for the trip. Cassie was trying to stay focused on the things that were exciting to her.

Sheila was just putting pancakes on a plate when Cassie walked into the kitchen.

Paul put his newspaper down. "Hey, Clompy!" he said, laughing.

"These boots take some getting used to!"

"Honey, we should have had you break them in more! Oh no, are you going to be okay in those?" Sheila asked, pulling syrup out of the fridge.

Paul got up then to help set the table.

"I'll be fine!" Cassie said. She poured herself some OJ and took a big gulp.

Sheila put a plate of pancakes in front of Cassie. Pancakes were one of Cassie's favorites.

"This is going to be a really good experience for you," Paul said, carefully applying butter to his pancakes.

"I know it is," Cassie said excitedly.

"I remember my first camping trip," he said. "It was really terrific. So much to see and explore."

"Wait, you've been camping? Why haven't we camped before as a family?" Cassie asked.

"Because I hate it now! All that mud and hiking and climbing! It's no fun at all!" Paul said, laughing.

"Paul, she's nervous about it. Don't tease her!" Sheila said. Just then, Cassie's mom got up from the table and opened the pantry door.

She pulled out a brown box.

"Cass," she said. "This is for you."

Cassie's face lit up. "Really? What is it?"

"It's from Erin. She asked that I give it to you right before you left."

Cassie took the box from her mother. It was addressed to Cassie, and the postmark was dated more than a week ago. "You had this for a week?" Cassie said, surprised.

Sheila laughed. "Yes! I am a very good secret keeper."

She was. Sheila was the inspiration for:

Life Rule #66: Secrets are forever. And ever.

Cassie pulled the tape up off the box, careful not to chip her Hard Candy Tantrum nails. She lifted off the top of the box and took out a small envelope. She laughed at Erin's note on it, written in her perfectly loopy handwriting:

I totally don't even know what this does. But every camper has to have one. xo! Erin!

Cassie lifted the seal of the envelope and peeked in. The prettiest purple twinkled inside. She pulled it out and looked at it. It was a carabiner — a kind of metal hook used for mountain climbing. Cassie had seen them in the L.L. Bean catalog. But this one was covered in gorgeous fuchsia crystals. Total GT!

"That is so lovely!" Sheila said.

Paul laughed. "Only my daughter would have sparkly camp gear."

In unison, Sheila and Cassie responded, "*Bejeweled* camp gear." They looked at each other and laughed.

"Here, Cass," Paul said. "You eat, and I'll put your keys on it."

"Thanks!" she said, passing the gift to Paul, her heart full of fuchsia love.

Before she could finish her breakfast, it was

time to go. Cassie kissed Sheila good-bye and Paul helped her load her stuff into the car.

On the way to school, Cassie pulled out her phone, so she could thank Erin for her fabulous present.

TY SO MUCH!! UR THE BEST BFF!! xo

Cassie smiled. They'd had a long talk on the phone last night — and Erin had never let on about the gift! Cassie didn't know what she would do without her. She was going to take all of Erin's wise advice and have a great camping trip.

As Paul pulled into the Oak Grove driveway, Cassie immediately saw the big yellow school bus, waiting for all of her classmates to pile on.

Before she got out of the car, Paul put his hand on her shoulder. "Cass," he said, his expression serious, "your mom and I are so proud of you, honey. You are going to have a great time."

Cassie smiled. "I know. Thanks, Dad." There were times when it felt better to call her parents "Mom" and "Dad." This was one of them.

"And, you know, if it's really bad and you want to come home, you can. There is nothing wrong with giving yourself a break."

He was right. Cassie knew that. But she wasn't planning to quit. This was going to be an opportunity to try something new and to maybe even *like* something new.

They hugged and got out of the car, Paul grabbing Cassie's bag for her.

"You take care, okay?" Paul said, walking her to the front door. He looked up at the school bus. "That old thing taking you to the site?" he asked.

"I think so."

"Well, don't worry about the camping trip then — you'll break down before you even get there."

They both laughed.

He handed Cassie her backpack and she grabbed it by the top handle, happy she didn't overpack *too* much. Once she got it on her back, Paul handed her the carabiner. Cassie stared at it blankly, not sure what to do with it. Paul pointed to his belt.

"Oh! Cool!" Cassie said, fastening it to her belt loop.

Paul shook his head at his daughter and smiled. "Okay, Cass! Have fun!" he said.

"I will. Thanks!" Cassie gave her dad a quick peck on the cheek and did an about-face. She was surprised she didn't fall flat on her face what with her new boots and the weight of her pack. Then she went inside to Mr. B's classroom to meet up with everyone.

By the time they were ready to board the bus, Cassie had eaten a granola bar, some trail mix, and shared a Gatorade with Etoile. Camping food was delicious!

Everyone was in a good mood and chatting away. Mary Ellen and her mom stood together, near the bus doors, saying "Hi" to each camper. Mary Ellen was introducing everyone to her mom; Cassie was petrified that Mrs. McGinty was going to be super-mean.

When Cassie and Etoile got to the front of the line, Mary Ellen hesitated for a moment and then introduced them to her mom.

Cassie was surprised to see Mrs. McGinty wearing a cool pair of jeans and a really chic khaki safari-ish shirt. She was even wearing makeup! Not too much, not too little, but she totally knew how to make her eyes pop! Her hair was tied back in a perfect twist.

"This is Etoile and Cassie," Mary Ellen said, unable to keep her smile on as she said it. "Cassie is the girl from Texas I was telling you about," she added, a mean flicker in her eyes.

Cassie nodded and smiled, practically shaking in her boots. She shook Mrs. McGinty's hand.

"This should be nothing for you, right?" Mary Ellen asked.

"What do you mean?" Cassie said, working hard at smiling back.

"I just thought that since you were from Texas and all, you were used to riding horses and rodeos and things like that, so camping should be easy. Right?" Mary Ellen said.

"I've actually never been on a horse," Cassie replied.

"Oh! I just thought that you rode horses because you wear cowboy boots," Mary Ellen said.

"I wear cowboy boots because they are fashionable. Not because I'm from Texas," Cassie said, feeling the smile on her face melt into a frown.

"You're the young lady from the fashion show?" Mrs. McGinty asked then.

Gulp.

Double gulp.

Even in all of her worrying, Cassie hadn't thought about the complete awkwardness of this moment.

Just as she was about to answer, Mr. Blackwell walked over. He wore broken-in jeans, a zip-up sweatshirt, and brown suede boots with thick red laces. Cassie had really seen all of these people in their finest at the Fash Bash, and she was pretty sure she was going to see them at their grungiest at The Gamut!

"You guys excited?" he asked.

Mary Ellen answered right away. "I can't wait! I was hoping that we could talk on the bus privately about the final night party," she added.

Cassie wondered what that party was going to be. She was excited for it and even smuggled a pair of cute pumps in her backpack for it.

"Sure, Mary Ellen," Mr. B said. "Let's get on the road and then we can talk. See you guys on the bus!" He moved down the line to greet the others.

"See you later!" Mary Ellen said.

Cassie and Etoile boarded the bus and settled in, seventh row on the right side, Etoile next to the window. Etoile always got the window seat because of her straight hair. If Cassie sat there, her curls would get blown into a bush-like frenzy!

"That was a close one," Cassie whispered about Mary Ellen and her mom.

"I know! I didn't know what to say when she asked about the Bash!" Etoile said.

As she slid into her seat Cassie saw Jonah and Seth Gordon sitting at the back of the bus. Cassie attempted to wave to them but Etoile stopped her;

she actually grabbed her hand before Cassie could get it waving!

"E!" Cassie squealed. "What are you doing?"

"Shhh!" Etoile practically hissed, pulling Cassie down into the seat. "It's nothing! I just don't want them to talk to us. Jonah is totally on my nerves." Etoile caught her breath and smoothed her hair.

"I was just going to say 'hello.'" Cassie settled into her seat. "You are super-weird sometimes!"

"*I'm* the weird one in this friendship?" Etoile exclaimed and looked at Cassie, smirking.

As they all settled in, PV climbed on board the bus. She was in her typical suit. Only today's was beige. Cassie wondered what her camp wear was going to look like.

PV clapped her hands three times to get everyone's attention. There was immediate silence, and PV cleared her throat. "Oak Grovians! What a special day this is. And what a wonderful time you have ahead of you. The joys of nature await. Keep your minds open, your heads high, and be sure to work together!"

She smiled at everyone, and Cassie smiled back. She didn't know what it was about them, but PV's speeches really rocked Cassie. She began to applaud, and everyone joined her.

"Good luck to you all!" PV turned then and thanked Mrs. McGinty and Mr. Blackwell. And with that, she walked down the stairs of the bus and into the school.

Cassie stared at Etoile. "Wait! PV's not coming?"

"No way. She would never really go camping." Etoile rolled her eyes.

Cassie stared out the window, her heart sinking, as she watching PV walk into the school.

Mary Ellen and her mother stood at the front of the bus then, waiting to address everyone. Cassie watched as Mary Ellen cleared her throat.

"Attention, everyone!" she shouted, her ponytail bopping behind her.

The bus quieted down, and all eyes turned to Mary Ellen.

"I think most of you have met my mom. She is the parent leader on the trip."

Mrs. McGinty smiled politely and waved.

Mary Ellen continued. "And, as you know, I am the student leader." She smiled. Everyone stared back at her blankly.

"So if you have any questions, please do not hesitate to ask either of us! Thank you!"

Everyone clapped, and Cassie joined in, trying hard to smile.

The bus started and before she knew it, they were driving deep into the woods of Maine, getting closer and closer to their adventure.

Cassie and Etoile had brought some Yearbook work to do on the bus. The Sports section had to be done. They'd printed out the contact sheets and flipped through them as the bus drove along.

Cassie looked at the photos, marking the ones she thought would be good additions. She came across one of Margery St. Maurice at the top of the cheerleading pyramid and she smiled. It was perfect. She had to show Etoile.

"E!" Cassie said, leaning over.

Etoile didn't budge. She sat there, staring, squinting her eyes. Cassie leaned forward to see what her friend was looking at. It was a sheet of pictures of Jonah and Seth and the rest of the soccer team, running off the soccer field, smiles so big, Cassie was sure they'd won the game. Their smiles totally made Cassie smile.

"That's an amazing picture!" she said, pointing.

Etoile jumped. "Huh? Oh, yeah. It's good." She flipped to the next page quickly.

"Are you okay?" Cassie asked.

"Yes, of course," Etoile whispered, running her hand over her flat sheet of chestnut hair.

Etoile only smoothed her hair like that when she was nervous.

Hmm? Cassie thought. *What's going on here? Was E crushing?!* Cassie knew for sure it couldn't be Jonah that Etoile liked. Was it Seth Gordon?

"E, what's up? That's a great picture."

Cassie *had* noticed that Etoile was acting a little strange lately around Jonah and Seth.

"Nothing," Etoile replied. "But you're right, it's a good picture. We should recommend it for the Sports spread."

Cassie raised one eyebrow.

Etoile cleared her throat. "Now let's get back to work," she said, clearly trying to be professional.

"Sure," Cassie said sweetly.

But this was not the end of this discussion. Cassie would make sure of it!

CHAPTER 5

Yikes!

After three hours of driving through the thick woods, the bus finally pulled through the gates of The Gamut. Cassie immediately took out her cell phone. She told Erin she would text her when they got there. But when Cassie looked at her phone, she was shocked to see she had no reception. None. Not even a glimmer of a bar!

Who can hear me now?

Cassie leaned over to Etoile. "I get no reception here!" she whispered.

Etoile pulled her phone out of her pocket. "Me neither. Wow, we are really in the middle of nowhere, huh?" she said, peering out the window.

That was the biggest difference between Cassie and Etoile. Etoile had grown up in Maine and didn't get weirded out by stuff like no reception or hiking or snowstorms in the spring. But Cassie had never dealt with anything like that in Houston! Humid bad-hair days, sure. But NO RECEPTION? That was just creepy!

Cassie decided to shut her phone off and put it away. There was nothing she could do about it now. She looked out the window as they drove through the front gates of The Gamut. It was very beautiful, all tall trees that reached up to the sky and soft dirt roads. The sunlight that cut through the branches was the warmest and yummiest yellow Cassie had ever seen. As the bus turned and twisted on the dirt road, Cassie could hear birds chirping everywhere.

"Wow! It's so nice here!" she said to Etoile, smiling.

"Totally," Etoile said, her face pressed against the window, taking it all in.

They pulled up to a big white wood building that had a hand-painted plaque on it that read MAIN HOUSE.

Mr. Blackwell stood to face everyone. "Welcome to The Gamut!" he said, smiling. "Please take a minute to gather up all your gear before getting off the bus. So, take a look around you, make sure you have it all, and then we'll head into the Main

48

House. We have a special welcome for you and we're going to begin our adventure right away."

Then Mary Ellen and her mother stood up to speak.

"Okay, guys, we want you in pairs. There are twenty-four of you, nice and even, so you can just stay with the person you're sitting with," Mrs. McGinty said, scanning the seats, making sure everyone had a partner.

Cassie looked at Etoile and smiled. What was the welcome that was planned? Cassie hoped it was a BBQ. She imagined burgers and hot dogs and coleslaw — and maybe even red gingham tablecloths!

"Okay, guys, let's go!" Mary Ellen said enthusiastically. She threw her right fist in the air, spun around, and bounded down the bus steps. Cassie had never seen her so excited.

As they waited for the people ahead of them to get off the bus, Cassie pulled out her mirror to check her hair and gloss. She was sure she was going to meet new people and she wanted to look her best.

New Life Rule!!! You have to work extra hard to look good when camping!

"Hey, Cassie," Jonah said from behind her.

Cassie turned around.

"Yes?" she responded tentatively, knowing he was going to kid her about something. It was always that way with Jonah.

"You know, you don't need lipstick for camping." He was smiling when he said it, and Cassie knew he was just being, well, himself.

Cassie laughed. "Um, first, genius, this is lip gloss," she pointed out, "and second, this is my *new* lip gloss!" She turned the tub over to show him. "Honeypot!"

Jonah and Seth started laughing hysterically.

"What?" Cassie said, knowing she wasn't *that* funny.

"I wouldn't want to wear something called 'honeypot' out in the woods. Dude, bears love honey!" Jonah said.

"Dude?" Cassie asked. As the boys continued to laugh, she rolled her eyes and turned to Etoile, who'd already clicked on her backpack. Then, Cassie had a sudden vision of being attacked by a big mama bear who wanted some cute gloss for her dry bear lips. Eek!

The line of campers began to walk off the bus ahead of them. Etoile followed.

Cassie quickly pulled on her backpack and clicked the strap around her waist, feeling very legitimate as she did so. She smiled proudly but then realized she still had to contend with her other little bag.

Suddenly bringing two bags didn't make any sense at all.

And neither did bringing Honeypot lip gloss.

When they all made it into the Main House, they met Craig Sanderson, the head counselor at The Gamut. He had gray hair and round glasses, and Cassie sort of thought he looked like her grandfather. He was dressed in cargo pants and a thick blue fleece zippie with a mountain embroidered on the sleeve. He seemed really energetic and enthusiastic, and he made Cassie feel safe.

Craig started his speech by shouting, "Welcome, campers!" and applauding. He then talked about how the entire group was going to leave this experience with a new understanding of themselves.

"The first thing I want to say to you all is please be safe and cautious while you are here. It's really important that you listen to me and your other counselors very closely."

Everyone nodded seriously, including Cassie.

"Let's never forget that we are in the deep woods and there are many wild animals who live here. Including black bears."

Cassie swallowed hard.

"We also only have electricity here in the Main House. Once we hike up to the campground, you will only have fire for light at night so we will really need you to stay close."

"And one final tip, guys," said Meghan, another one of the counselors, "keep the group together. There's safety in numbers." Meghan was in a similar outfit to Craig's, except her zippie was dark green.

Cassie shifted a little under the weight of her backpack. She couldn't wait to put it down. Suddenly, everything felt so real. Too real maybe.

Craig gave them a quick tour of the Main House and told them that they would all return there for the celebration on the final night. Craig also mentioned that if someone needed medical attention, they would be brought to the Main House.

Cassie had to stop herself from asking how often that happened. Instead, she reached her hand over to Etoile's and squeezed.

Etoile tried her best to keep Cassie calm. "It's totally fine," she mouthed.

"Now, guys," Craig said, "follow me. We're gonna start our first hike to the campsite. As we leave, I want you each to take a water bottle and two granola bars from the table, and load them into your packs." He pointed to a table, near the door. "Please do not drink too much water or eat the bars. We don't want you cramping. Keep them in your packs, just in case."

Just in case?! Cassie couldn't believe her ears. Hiking? Already? Weren't they there to learn how to hike? Maybe she wasn't ready for this. Were any of them? She looked around the group for terrified faces but everyone actually looked happy. How were they not freaked out about all of this?

Just in case what?!

Cassie's eyes met Mary Ellen's, who was standing next to her mother, practically glowing. She had her arms crossed and was nodding her head very seriously at everything Craig was saying.

When Mary Ellen noticed Cassie, her eyes grew big and a smirk curved on her lips. She must have thought this was all SO funny — and she seemed SO sure that the girl from Texas would never be able to survive this kind of a thing.

But the problem was, this time, Cassie wondered if she was right.

CHAPTER 6

Yikes x A Squillion!

The first few minutes of the hike didn't seem too bad. If Cassie tuned out all of the terrifying things that Craig and other counselors were talking about, like the poisonous berries they were walking past, she was okay. But, why would anyone want to hike and sleep in a place with poison and wild animals? And why would someone even want to talk about those kinds of things?

Cassie kept her head down as they walked on the dirt path. Her boots still felt like they were too heavy as she clomped along. Etoile was right in front of her, and Cassie followed her friend's every footstep, over roots, around bushes, through puddles.

After about half an hour, Cassie found her confidence and stride. She looked around at the lush green leaves and the beautiful birds that darted in and out of trees. The group slowed down and finally stopped, right near a wide stream. Cassie thought the sound of the water washing over the rocks was calming.

Craig and Mr. B gathered everyone near the water.

"This is so pretty," Cassie said to Etoile.

"I know!" Etoile said, looking at the water.

"Okay, everyone," Craig said, his voice almost getting lost in the sound of the water. "We are now about twenty minutes from the site."

Twenty minutes? This isn't the site? Cassie thought, her bags growing heavier by the moment.

After Craig had seen her struggling with them in the Main House, he had helped Cassie latch the small one to the big one, using her new bejeweled carabiner.

"Oh, neat! Is that what it's for?" Cassie had asked.

Craig had laughed. "I've never seen one like this," he'd said, clipping Cassie's bags together.

"It's a one of a kind!" she'd replied.

Craig had settled the packs onto her back. "Well, it sounds right for a one-of-a-kind young lady," he had chuckled. "But didn't anyone tell you to bring just one bag?" he had asked knowingly.

"To be honest, Craig," Cassie had said politely, "we're sort of lucky that I didn't pack four bags, like I thought I should."

"Good point," Craig had said.

Now Craig was addressing the group.

"In order to get to the site, we need to cross this water," he said, pointing his thumb behind him. "You have two choices. You can cross the stream, carefully walking from stone to stone. Or you can climb up to that fallen tree," he pointed above, at a thick tree trunk that stretched above the stream, about five feet above them, "and walk across it."

Cassie thought she was going to pass out. Both options seemed terrible! She took a deep breath and raised her hand. When Craig saw her, he nodded. "We have a question from the girl with two backpacks." He laughed a little at his own joke. And everyone else went right along with him.

Super, Cassie thought.

Another deep breath. "Well, I was wondering if you have a recommendation about which one we should do."

"That's a great question. But it's one that I am not going to answer. Being here at The Gamut, you all need to make these kinds of decisions on your own."

Super-duper. Making decisions on her own was nothing new for Cassie, really. But making life-or-death decisions certainly was!

Craig continued. "If you decide to cross the rocks, you should know that they are slippery and you're going to really have to be careful. But the water isn't very deep in this area. Up to your knees or so. The current can be strong, so it could disrupt your balance." He stopped for a moment and laughed. "And get ready for some very cold water if you fall in."

Cassie leaned in to Etoile. "This is funny?" she whispered.

Craig continued. "And if you decide to climb across" — he stopped and looked up above them at the long, solid-looking, fallen tree stretched across the water — "it's not too narrow, so you can easily walk it — but you have to be prepared to haul your gear and keep your footing. There is a rope up above to hold on to."

A chill ran down Cassie's spine. *Climb across that thing, holding on to a rope, dangling miles above the earth? No thank you!*

Cassie raised her hand again. Craig stopped and smiled. "Yes . . ." he said, clearly waiting for her name.

"Cassie," Cassie said firmly.

"Yes, Cassie?"

"Are there any other choices?" She was kidding, of course, but she had to ask, just in case.

Craig laughed and everyone around her giggled.

"No, there's not. But I will say this: Any of the choices we present you with here are safe. They are tried-and-true methods that many people have accomplished successfully. The staff is here to help you all, so never hesitate to ask for it." Craig smiled. "When you've made your decisions, please line up. Water people over here," he pointed behind him. "And tree people over there." He motioned to a spot in front of the tree, where Meghan was standing.

Quickly, people divided up. Cassie was surprised to see how easily everyone made their decisions.

Etoile leaned in to Cassie. She was one of the very few people who knew that Cassie was afraid of heights. Not totally afraid — but afraid enough that tiptoeing across a branch definitely qualified as a no-no.

"I'll do whichever one you want to do," Etoile said.

Cassie knew that Etoile was going to be there for her every step of the way but wanted her to make her own choices, too. "I think you should do the tree if you want. Seriously. I'm going to do the water."

"No! I'll do the water, too," Etoile exclaimed, ever the supportive friend.

"Etoile, you straightened your hair this morning. I know you. You will freak if it frizzes up this early in the trip." Cassie was worried about her hair, too, but she was just going to have to get over that. With the choices given, the water was the only way to go.

"You're sure?" Etoile asked.

"No. Are you, though?"

"Nope." Etoile put her arm around Cassie's shoulders and gave her a quick hug. "I'll be looking out for you from up there!" Etoile said.

"Just keep your eyes on where you're stepping. I'll be fine!"

"Okay, you too!" Etoile straightened her glasses, adjusted her backpack, and joined the tree group.

Standing there, between the two groups, Cassie felt all eyes on her. She took another deep breath and joined the water group. Mr. B was standing at the front of the line and that made Cassie feel good. He gave her a quick thumbs-up.

"All right, everyone, good luck. Listen to your counselors and most of all, have fun!" Craig said.

Cassie decided to ignore his last words. Eating cheese fries and paging through mags with Etoile was fun.

But *this*? This was *not* fun.

In a matter of seconds, Cassie was walking with her group to the edge of the water. She started to notice a cramp in her calf and felt herself panicking a little bit. There was so much to worry about. Just then, the water picked up speed and rushed past them. It looked cold. And wet. And Cassie was sure there were tons of creepy things living in it. She looked back at the tree group, heading toward their climb. She reconsidered her decision for a moment. But no, the water was the way to go. Cassie sent a good vibe to Etoile and then focused on what she had to do. If she was going to make it across the water, she would have to calm down and focus.

"All right," Craig shouted to the group. "Please cross with a partner. You should stay side by side the whole way. The rocks are wide enough."

Mr. B let some of the group pass him, until he and Cassie were standing at the edge of the water together.

"Will you be my partner?" he asked.

"Sure!" Cassie said, relieved to have an adult with her.

"You doing okay?" he asked, his eyes bright and supportive.

"I've been better, maybe. But I'm okay!" Cassie said.

Before it was their turn, Cassie adjusted her backpack and tightened the straps around her waist. She pulled up her jeans and tucked them into her boots to keep them dry.

"Ready?" Mr. Blackwell asked.

"Totally," Cassie said, her best game-face on.

They took a step forward together. Getting to the first rock seemed easy. It was long and flat and close to the water's edge. With her foot right at the edge of the water, the ground a little soft underneath her, she stepped on the rock with her left foot. With a slight slip in the mud, she followed with her right foot and was secure on the rock.

She looked ahead of her and saw that everyone was taking it slow, which was a relief.

"Okay, next one," Mr. B said, looking out ahead of him.

Cassie examined the next rock. It was a little farther away but not too much. It was mostly flat like the current one. But the water was hitting it harder, so she was going to have to step carefully. She took a moment to dig through her jacket pocket for an elastic. She had to tie her curls back and out of the way.

"Here goes," Mr. B said.

He took a big step forward and made it to the rock safely. He turned to Cassie. "That was easier than it looks!"

"Great!" she called to him. Although it didn't feel great. Her leg was still feeling crampy.

She stepped to the very edge of the rock and put her hands out to the side. She pushed forward, her right leg stretching across the water and settling on the rock. She waited just one sec to get her balance and then brought her other leg over.

"Yay!" she said happily. But when she looked up at Mr. B, he didn't look happy. He was looking at the next rock. This one was really far away! There was no way they could actually make it across in one step.

"How do we do that?" he asked, looking out.

"I don't know. You're the teacher!" she said, panic rumbling in her stomach.

They stared out for a moment. They hadn't been paying enough attention to the groups ahead of them to see how they did it.

As she looked out ahead of her, she saw another stone, this one much smaller, that was definitely within stepping distance. It was sort of underwater but not too deep.

"What about that rock?" Cassie asked, pointing to her discovery.

Mr. Blackwell looked. "Oh, yeah!" he said.

"But I don't think it's going to get us close enough," Cassie said.

"Maybe there's another that you can see when you're out there. I'm going to look."

Cassie watched as Mr. B carefully stepped over to the small rock. Once he was there, the water rushing over his feet, he shouted, "Yes! There's two more rocks on the way! C'mon!" He waved to Cassie to follow him.

Proud for a moment, Cassie waited as Mr. B stepped to the second rock and then followed right behind him. The water ran over her feet, but she was safe in her RedHeads!

She stepped onto the next small rock and then finally onto the large rock, joining Mr. B, ready to solve the next piece of the puzzle.

Fifteen minutes — and five more rocks later — Cassie and Mr. B had almost made it to the other side of the water. As Cassie waited for him to step off the final rock, she looked up. She'd heard some people above her, as they crossed the tree. And when she looked up, she was amazed by what she saw! People were actually walking across the tree trunk, hands above them, holding on to a rope for more balance. She looked for Etoile and saw that she was almost at the other side. Cassie was certain her friend was calm and collected. Yay for Etoile! She did it!

Cassie looked back at her last step and refocused. She adjusted her pack once more and took her last step, onto dry land finally! But as she did, the water surged and washed over the rock with more force than she was expecting.

Suddenly — and before she could even realize it — her foot slipped off the rock.

Life Rule #39: If it can happen, it probably will!

Before Cassie knew it, she was in midair. And as she tried to regain her footing, her heavy backpack weighed her down. She slammed into the wet, muddy riverbank, butt first.

For a second, Cassie had no idea what happened. Sitting in sludge, stunned, she saw a small group of people gather. The counselors knelt down over her.

Mary Ellen's BFF, Lynn Bauman, ran over. "Cassie, are you okay?"

She was okay. Just wet and muddy. All over her new camping jeans, too!

She didn't know what to do, so she just starting laughing. "I'm totally fine!" she said, through her giggling.

The counselors helped her up. Finally on her feet, Cassie looked out at the rest of the water group and her cheeks flushed with embarrassment.

"Oops!" she said.

No one had a response. They just turned away, whispering to one another.

Mr. B smiled. "You okay?"

Cassie wondered if there were any creepy-crawlies on her somewhere. She nervously brushed herself off. "I'm fine," she said.

"Hey, we made it! That's pretty cool!" he said.

Cassie smiled. He was right. But still, she wasn't feeling too glamorous, with mud all over her pants. She sighed.

Nature: 1. Cassie: 0.

CHAPTER 7

Just Keep Movin', Girl

Cassie did her best to keep her spirits high, even though she felt gross in her muddy jeans. But she pushed on, dreading the moment when the water group would meet up with the tree group. Mary Ellen and her mother had led the tree group, and Cassie didn't think she could deal with any negative comments.

As they walked, her bags seemed to grow heavier with each and every step. She didn't want to admit it but she was secretly relieved that she hadn't brought too many clothes — or magazines. It would have been impossible to carry everything for so long!

As they rounded a turn on the hiking path, Craig spoke. "Hey, guys," he said, "we're just about there." He stopped for a moment. "And our timing is impeccable because I hear the tree group coming."

Everyone turned to look and sure enough, their fellow campers came marching up another path. When Cassie saw Etoile walking a few feet behind Jonah and Seth, she knew her friend must have spent the entire time trying to avoid them.

Oh, that girl! Cassie thought, forgetting about her muddy jeans for the first time since her fall.

Of course, Mary Ellen was leading the pack, holding what seemed to be a newfound walking stick.

Cassie fought to keep her eyes from rolling.

Mary Ellen made a beeline over to Cassie, her eyes widening as she got closer.

"So, how did the stream go?" she asked, a satisfied smile curled on her lips.

"It was great!" Cassie said, trying her hardest to sound upbeat.

"Yeah. I can see that." Mary Ellen eyed Cassie's mud-caked jeans.

Etoile was right behind Mary Ellen.

"Hey!" she said to Cassie. "You made it! Go you!"

"It was great! Well, until I totally bit it and fell in the mud."

Etoile and Cassie laughed together. Mary Ellen

stood, scowling. Mrs. McGinty came over then, her face concerned.

"Cassie! Mr. Blackwell told me you fell! Honey, are you all right?" Her eyes were big and kind. Just then, Cassie realized that Mary Ellen looked a lot like her mother.

"I'm okay. Thank you. I didn't get hurt at all. Just sort of muddy."

"That's why I hate that rule about two pairs of pants. It just seems too few for a trip a like this," Mrs. McGinty said, smiling.

Maybe Mary Ellen's mom was nicer than Cassie thought she was.

"When we get settled in, I can help you clean those jeans up," she said.

Mary Ellen's face twisted in anger. "Mother! We have things to do when we get to the site that are going to take a lot of your time."

Etoile jumped right in. "Don't worry about it. I can help Cassie. That's what friends are for." Etoile grabbed Cassie's arm and led her away, Cassie thanking Mrs. McGinty for her concern.

"I don't know what the deal is with that Mary Ellen sometimes," Etoile said. "She really needs to get over it though!"

They walked toward the rest of the group and

headed into the campground. Cassie was surprised to see what it actually looked like. She'd imagined the worst of the worst, of course. Beehives and bears and poison ivy and snakes and stuff. But what she saw was better than what she'd hoped for. It was hardly glamorous, hardly had the comforts of home, but it was kind of nice!

The site was a large stretch of land, with tons of big trees that seemed to turn greener and greener the more Cassie looked at them. There was a central area with a fire pit for cooking, with some picnic tables set up nearby. There was something kind of cute about it all. But the cuteness ended when Cassie got a look at the girls' bathroom. The shower stalls were yellowed and dingy, and she was sure that the water was going to be freezing. She didn't even let herself look at the bathroom stalls.

"It's good," Etoile said as convincingly as possible.

"Well, it's certainly not Chez Cassie, but it will do," Cassie responded, clasping Etoile's hand in hers.

Once they'd had a chance to put down their packs and get a quick tour, Craig told them their next activity would be to build their tents. He explained that having a place to sleep was very important on a trip like this so he wanted to make sure that they all had one as soon as possible. There were piles of nylon-bagged tents stacked up in the center of the site. Craig handed one to each pair of campers. Cassie had her eye on a particularly stunning Kelly green one and was thrilled when it was handed to them.

Maybe my luck is changing! she thought.

Once everyone had their tents, Craig and the counselors built their own, explaining how they did it, step-by-step. Cassie and Etoile paid close attention. Cassie was even trying to make up a few rhymes while she listened, so she'd be able to remember the steps more easily. She did this with her homework all the time, although it was a real challenge with pre-al.

The groundsheet is neat to keep the rain off our feet. . . .

The stakes make sure we stay in place. . . .

When the demonstration was complete, Cassie was amazed at how awesome the tents looked. She was excited to start hers with Etoile and wondered if she and Etoile could make some sort of leaf collage to hang inside!

Everyone paired up quickly and walked to the tent area. Lynn and Mary Ellen were going to share a tent. Deirdre and Margery followed right behind them. Of course, Jonah and Seth and the rest of the boys all went to their own area. Cassie and Etoile walked to the spot next to Margery and Deirdre's tent. They dropped their backpacks, each comparing the weight of the other's — and each convinced that her pack was the heavier one.

"You guys doing okay?" Margery asked kindly.

"I think so," Cassie said.

The two groups carefully unpacked their tents, placing all of the pieces in front of them. Once they were unpacked, they got to work.

Or, at least, Cassie and Etoile tried to.

Even though Cassie was reciting her tent poems aloud, she still couldn't figure out what any of the poems really meant. Etoile wasn't much help either. She just stood there, hands on her hips, adjusting her glasses on the bridge of her nose every now and then.

When the girls finally realized they needed to feed one of the poles into one side of the tent, Cassie couldn't keep her poor, tired arms from trembling. Lugging that backpack really had been hard work! But the final straw came when Etoile got distracted for a moment and tripped and fell into the tent, knocking the whole thing over! Cassie wouldn't say it out loud, but she was secretly relieved: It felt good to be with someone who was as clumsy as she was!

Once their completely doubled-over laughing fit subsided, the girls looked around for a counselor who would be able to help them. As they waited for help, Cassie told Etoile the whole long story about how she'd fallen off the rock earlier. Etoile laughed so much that she actually snorted. Right when they were in the middle of another laughing fit, Mary Ellen walked over from her tent.

"Is something funny?" she asked a little snidely, Cassie thought.

"Cassie was just telling me about a mishap!" Etoile said.

Cassie smiled when she realized that Etoile wasn't going to mention Cassie's fall to Mary Ellen.

"Oh," Mary Ellen said, her nose crinkling, "you mean when you fell earlier today?"

Both girls stopped laughing. It was clear Mary Ellen was not going to be nice about the whole thing.

"You know," Mary Ellen continued, "this is really serious stuff. And you shouldn't be standing here laughing. You guys are the only ones who haven't gotten your tent up yet, if you haven't noticed."

Just when Cassie and Etoile thought the rant was all over, Mary Ellen continued, "You have to work on this trip. Sorry to say it, but it's true." Mary Ellen adjusted the hood of her sweatshirt, squinted her eyes, and turned from them.

As she walked away, Cassie didn't know what to do. She *was* trying hard. She really was. But they had to have fun along the way, too.

Right?

CHAPTER 8

Wrong!

That night, they had an astronomy lesson under the stars, and Cassie couldn't believe how big and beautiful the dark blue sky was. She'd never seen stars like that before! In Houston, there were some stars to see, but sitting on the ground in the middle of the woods in Maine was a totally different story! It was more beautiful than any planetarium Cassie had ever seen, that was for sure.

Craig pointed out the North Star and the Big and Little Dippers. And then, right in the middle of talking, he interrupted himself to point out a shooting star. Cassie had never seen one of those before. She wished she had reception on her phone so she could update Erin on everything — even her muddy jeans!

As she sat and listened, Jonah leaned over.

"Hey, Knight," he said.

"What's up?"

"How's that honey lip gloss? Any bears try to kiss you yet?"

Cassie rolled her eyes but got nervous about a black bear trying to give her a kiss in the middle of the night. Could that happen?

"Would you leave her alone?!" Etoile said, giving Jonah a push.

Seth leaned over then. "C'mon, man. Listen to this, it's really interesting," he said, pointing at the sky. "Hey, Etoile," he said, smiling.

Etoile didn't say anything back. She just shook her head, like she always did.

Hoping to fill the silence, Cassie said, "You know 'etoile' means 'star' in French?"

Seth smiled again. "Cool!"

"Yeah, yeah, she's a star. Great," Jonah said.

Seth elbowed Jonah and pointed up to the sky.

Jonah obeyed his friend and looked up.

When Cassie looked at Etoile, her friend was practically ghost-colored. Cassie grabbed Etoile's hand and squeezed it, giving her friend a big smile. "You're a star," she whispered.

Etoile smiled and they both looked up at the vast sky.

As Craig continued on with the lesson, Cassie got drowsy. The fresh night air was getting colder by the second. She yawned a big, exhausted yawn and realized that most people around her were doing the very same thing.

Craig finished his talking soon after that. "Okay, everyone," he said, "I think it's time to turn in. Thanks for a great first day, and we'll see you bright and early in the morning."

"Breakfast is at 6:30, everyone, so make sure you get some sleep," Mr. Blackwell added.

The sleepy campers walked to their tents and got ready for bed.

When Cassie and Etoile had settled into their cozy sleeping bags, they whispered to each other for a while.

"Did you have an okay day today?" Etoile whispered.

"You mean besides falling down and humiliating myself?" Cassie asked, only half kidding.

"Besides that, yes," Etoile said, giggling a little.

"I think it was an okay day." Cassie stared up at the top of the tent, trying her best to ignore what felt like an enormous tree root sticking into her back.

She could hear chirping and buzzing coming from the trees outside the tent. Bugs! She began to think about the fact that there was only a little piece of nylon separating her from all those creepy-crawlies.

"It sounds like there are a lot of bugs out there, huh?" Cassie asked, trying her best not to sound scared.

But there was no response from Etoile. In just that one second, she had fallen asleep, leaving Cassie alone.

Alone with all those bugs! Cassie swallowed hard. She did her best not to think about it, and she closed her eyes, trying to focus on remembering the beautiful night sky they'd all just looked at with Craig. But she wasn't feeling tired anymore. Now, Cassie felt wide awake. Wide awake . . . and scared.

Little by little, she was able to calm herself down and she slowly started to doze. She was pretty exhausted and knew she had a big day tomorrow.

SNAP!

Cassie shot straight up. *What was that?* she wondered. It sounded like a branch cracking. Cassie couldn't imagine what would be walking through the woods at night. A raccoon? A bat? Did bats walk?

Maybe a black bear?

Or, worse, Bigfoot?!

Cassie was panicked. "E!" she whispered.

Etoile made some kind of sleepy sound but didn't wake up.

"E!" Cassie whispered again. It was more like a whisper-scream this time.

Etoile shot up out of her sleep, eyes wild.

"What?!" she asked.

Cassie instantly felt dumb for waking Etoile up.

"Sorry. It's nothing. I just heard a sound or something," Cassie said, blushing.

"Oh, okay. Don't worry, there's nothing out there. Just try and get some sleep," Etoile murmured, already half asleep again. She put her head back down and fell right back to sleep.

Cassie tried her best to calm down. She put her head on her pillow and squeezed her eyes closed, trying to breath slowly. Morning could not come soon enough. There were so many places she wanted to be other than camping. She wondered what her parents were doing. And what was going on with her friends in Texas. She listened for more snapping sounds and finally decided that she had no other choice than to count sheep in order to get to sleep.

*   *   *

By the time morning came, Cassie was exhausted. She'd gotten some sleep but not nearly enough. And the thought of trying to wake herself up in those dingy showers made her feel even more exhausted and gross.

But after she showered and got dressed, she felt a little bit better.

After carefully applying her sunscreen and bug spray, Cassie walked over to breakfast with Etoile, Jonah, Seth, and some of their other tent neighbors. She was relieved that, at the very least, the first dreadful day was behind her.

"It would be so good if there were pancakes for breakfast," Cassie said to Etoile.

From behind her, Jonah responded, "I don't think we're going to get pancakes. We're in the woods."

Cassie rolled her eyes and imagined Sheila's delicious pancakes with syrup and butter. Yum!

When they got to the tables, Craig and the other counselors were cooking over the fire.

"Morning, campers!" he called.

"Morning!" some people responded.

"Have a seat! The oatmeal is ready," Craig said, sticking a big ladle into the pot on the fire.

Cassie loved oatmeal, with oodles of brown

sugar and cinnamon. Perfect! But when the metal cup was put down in front of her, Cassie was disappointed to find a mass of thick gooeyness inside it. She could barely poke a spoon into it.

"Sorry, Cassie," Mary Ellen said from across the table. "I heard you wanted pancakes," she added, grinning.

Determined not to seem defeated, Cassie smiled. "No, this is great! I love oatmeal!" She took a spoonful and shoved it into her mouth, trying not to twist her face in disgust as she tasted the pasty wretchedness.

After they ate, Cassie went back to her tent, determined to scrub the mud out of her jeans. She had wanted to clean them last night but by the time they ate and got settled in, she was way too tired to do anything else. But being stuck with only one clean pair of pants for three days gave the phrase "fashion emergency" a whole new meaning.

Mrs. McGinty even came to find Cassie after breakfast to ask if she was okay.

"Are you girls settling in?" she asked Cassie and Etoile as she walked toward their tent area.

Cassie was sitting in front of the tent, examining her jeans, while Etoile got ready for the day. Cassie knew she shouldn't have let them sit overnight but she hadn't had a choice. Sleep was sometimes more important than fashion!

Normally, she would have made a joke about how she wasn't okay because of her jeans but she didn't want Mrs. McGinty to think she was shallow. So, she decided on, "We're okay! Just need to do some laundry." It seemed stupid as it came out of her mouth — she didn't sound like herself.

"Let me see those," Mrs. McGinty said, holding out her hands. When she did, Cassie noticed she had short — but manicured — nails, polished with just a hint of pink.

Cassie passed the jeans over, sad that they might stay stained forever.

"How could you say you're okay when a fabulous pair of classic Levi's have been dragged through the mud!" Mrs. McGinty said, winking at Cassie.

Cassie's heart soared. She sprung up to stand next to Mrs. McGinty.

"Well, you know, I have some stain remover in my bag. We could try to get some of the mud out with that," Mary Ellen's mom said, squinting at the jeans.

"Really?" Cassie asked, shocked. She hadn't expected her to say that, especially since it wasn't on the list of what they could take on the trip.

"Sure. Let's take a walk and see what we can do. I bet we can get this out."

"Okay!" Cassie said excitedly. She ran to the tent and stuck her head through the door flap. Inside, Etoile had put her iPod on, bopping her head. She was straightening out stuff in her backpack.

"E!" Cassie whispered excitedly.

Etoile took one of her earbuds out. "Any luck?"

"Not yet. But Mary Ellen's mom is taking me to her tent to get some stain remover!"

Etoile raised an eyebrow.

"That's so sweet, right?" Cassie asked.

"Sounds like a McGinty scheme, if you ask me," Etoile said.

"Oh, please." Cassie dismissed Etoile's joke. "I'll be back soon."

"Okay," Etoile smiled. "Good luck!"

Cassie walked back out to Mrs. McGinty and the two headed over to her tent.

A half hour later, Cassie's jeans had been treated, rinsed, and then actually beaten against a rock. They were as good as new. Cassie couldn't believe her luck! As she and Mrs. McGinty walked back to the main campground, they got to know each other a little bit. Cassie was amazed to find out that Mrs. McGinty was once an editor for a New York City newspaper. And for the style section, no less!

"Style is everything," Mrs. McGinty said, laughing.

"I totally know what you mean," Cassie agreed, carefully walking over the big roots of a tree.

"But it has to be about you, about who you are — not about what someone tells you you're supposed to be or look like." Mrs. McGinty looked at Cassie and smiled.

"I know what you mean," Cassie said seriously.

"I know you do. You've got great style, Cassie!" she said, smiling. "Mary Ellen never told you what I did in New York?" Mrs. McGinty asked then, casually.

"No," Cassie said, knowing Mary Ellen would never have told her something like that, especially after how angry Mary Ellen had been about the Fash Bash. Cassie wondered if Mrs. McGinty knew that she and Mary Ellen didn't always get along.

As they walked into the campsite, everyone was getting ready for their next activity: white-water rafting. Cassie was petrified.

"Are you ready to raft?" Mrs. McGinty asked excitedly.

"NO!" Cassie exclaimed. "I'm really scared."

"Don't be, it's going to be fun and we're going to make sure you are safe."

Hearing Mrs. McGinty say that made Cassie feel a lot better. As they walked, Cassie saw Mary Ellen standing with her friends on the other side of the camp. When Mary Ellen noticed Cassie and her mother walking together, her face squinched up, angry. Mrs. McGinty saw Mary Ellen, too, and called her over to them. Mary Ellen obeyed her mother but walked slowly, her face twisting tighter and tighter with each step.

Cassie wasn't ready for this. She still was reeling over everything she'd learned about Mrs. McGinty.

"Mary Ellen," Mrs. McGinty said as she approached them, "I can't believe you didn't tell Cassie that I used to work for the style section!" She wasn't angry, but she sounded surprised.

"Oh, it just never came up," Mary Ellen said casually. "Mom, it's almost time to head to the rafting site, we should hurry."

Mrs. McGinty looked at her watch. "Oh, it is! Sorry!" she said to Mary Ellen. Mrs. McGinty turned to Cassie. "Go get your stuff and we'll see you in a few minutes, honey," she said.

Cassie smiled, her heart full of warmth. "Okay, I will! Thanks again for helping me get these clean!" She held up her wet jeans. Then she smiled at both Mary Ellen and her mom, and ran to her tent. Cassie couldn't believe how cool Mrs. McGinty was! She always knew Mary Ellen had to be okay, deep down — and now this proved it!

The rafting site was farther away than Cassie thought it was going to be. They hiked for about an hour, over lots of big, fallen trees and soft, squishy land. The cramp found its way back into Cassie's leg as they walked. She felt her back perspiring, her hair wilting. All she could think about was a good, hot shower and some lip gloss. And it was still only morning!

As the group walked, the counselors stopped every now and again to point out different trees and plants. They even stopped once when one of the counselors saw a bunch of worms wriggling near a tree stump. When the counselors picked up one of the worms, some campers did the same and they watched them wriggle on their hands as the counselor explained that they were probably feeding on the rotting wood.

It took all of Cassie's strength to not whip out her insect spray and spritz everything in sight! Of course, Jonah decided to torture poor Etoile and chased her around with a creepy worm in his hand. Etoile was really angry but Cassie and Seth couldn't help but laugh at it all.

Then, before she really knew what was happening, Cassie found herself lined up and waiting with all of her classmates at a dock; they were all wearing orange life vests and gumball-blue helmets. She was trying her hardest to ignore the fact that these colors were absolutely horrific with her hair and skin tone. But she was trying even harder to not absolutely, positively freak out.

The rafts were big, bright yellow rubber boats. She sat and watched as kids were sent to different ones, some of them looking as nervous as she felt. There were eight students and two adults in each raft, and somehow Cassie was given a front seat. Cassie watched as Jonah and Seth were sent to the same raft, and she hoped that Etoile might make it onto hers.

Etoile was up next and Cassie watched as the counselor looked at each raft, trying to figure out where to send her. She then pointed at Cassie's raft, and Etoile's face lit up.

Cassie waved from her seat as Etoile climbed on. The girls' eyes met — a look of pure terror on their faces — and they both smiled, relieved they were together. And then, before Cassie had another thought, their raft was being pushed out into the water. Craig was in the back, steering.

"Okay, everyone, forward paddle!" he yelled. Cassie couldn't believe someone was actually yelling the word "paddle" — and at her, no less!

She stuck her oar in the water and pushed it through, the way she'd been instructed to earlier. She wasn't at all convinced that they would really get themselves moving but sure enough, they coasted out into the river and the slight current pushed them forward.

"Great job!" Craig yelled behind them.

They paddled and paddled for about fifteen minutes, the waters calm and clear, the sun strong above them. Once Cassie found the rhythm of it all, she let herself relax a little. She glanced back to see how Etoile was doing. She looked really focused. Etoile had an awesome ability — she could let her fears go and totally concentrate. She did it in her fashion design; she did it in her life. Cassie beamed at her friend, who was sweating, rowing, and loving every minute of it. Etoile was sheer inspiration to Cassie.

Craig shouted to the group. "Okay, you all, we're moving into rougher waters. Nothing to worry about but you'll need to listen closely to me. Okay?"

No one answered.

"Okay?" Craig shouted loudly.

Everyone responded then. "Okay!"

"There we go. This is all about good communication, you guys! And teamwork!"

Cassie smiled at Etoile. They knew a lot about teamwork.

Suddenly, Craig shouted, "LEFT! Left paddle!"

Snapped back to the reality of being a little redhead in a big, blue river, Cassie whipped her head around to face forward and paddle as she was instructed to do. She dug her paddle into the water and they moved to the right. There was a little bit of a dip in front of them suddenly, and Cassie braced herself for a bumpy ride.

"FORWARD PADDLE!" Craig shouted.

Cassie's heart began to race. The sound of the water was getting louder and louder and as they came to the dip, Cassie could see that there were a lot more ahead of them. And a few waterfalls!

Cassie couldn't believe it. She would never have done something like this in Houston. She didn't even *know* stuff like this existed when she lived in Houston!

They went over the first dip, and Cassie's stomach flipped inside of her as they splashed back into the water.

"FORWARD PADDLE! Faster!"

The oars hit the water hard and fast, and soon, they were splashing up and down, hurtling down the river. Cassie's heart was racing as she struggled to keep up the pace.

Just then, she heard Craig shout again. Only this time, they were three of the scariest words she'd ever heard:

"CASSIE, WATCH OUT!"

Cassie looked quickly to the left and right, certain that a bear or a shark or a horde of bees was closing in on her. But then, when she looked in front of her, she knew exactly what Craig was yelling about.

Cassie thought hard, hoping she could find a life rule for this situation.

But there was no life rule for *this*!

The raft was heading straight toward an enormous drop. Before they boarded the rafts, Craig had told the group that they'd go over a few drops. But, Cassie never imagined it would be so *real*!

Putting all of her faith in her Pantene, Cassie paddled forward, her eyes locked on to where the water seemed to disappear over the side of the rocks.

"Paddle!"

Again, the oars hit the water hard. Cassie quickly

pulled at the chinstrap of her helmet, and she dug her paddle into the water.

"PADDLE!"

The water rushed against them, speeding them up, faster and faster.

And then, suddenly, there she was: paddle in the air, at the edge of the drop. Cassie's eyes widened as she took it all in. The water rushed out in front of her. And beneath them, more bumpy rapids, more waterfalls — and then farther up ahead, it all looked calm and peaceful.

She felt the raft tip forward.

"Pull your oars in!" Craig yelled.

Cassie pulled her oar in and clasped her hands together over it, tight on her lap. She wished she could hold Etoile's hand right then, but the old oar would have to do! She squeezed her eyes shut and they tumbled forward, the raft suspended in the air, the water rushing past them. They tumbled forward and Cassie let out a roller coaster–worthy scream.

BANG!

The raft slapped into the current again, startling Cassie. She opened her eyes. All she could see was an enormous sheet of water headed toward her.

She screamed more as the water slapped against her and covered the raft in an icy splash.

The raft was drenched. Cassie was breathless. And soaked!

She felt like she wanted to cry but she wasn't sure why exactly. At first, she thought it was because of her dripping hair and wet clothes. But then, she quickly realized that it wasn't that at all. Cassie was exhilarated, happier than she might have ever been in her entire life.

And before she could stop herself, she threw her fists in the air and pumped them furiously.

"Whoo-hoo!!" Cassie screamed gloriously, her voice echoing against the rocks around them. She looked behind her and saw all of her classmates cheering. Etoile's helmet was smushed down on her head, but Cassie saw her pearly whites.

"Paddles out! Forward paddle!" Craig screamed again.

Cassie jammed her paddle into the water, soaking wet. Feeling gross never felt so good!

CHAPTER 9

Obstacles, Obstacles Everywhere!

Cassie woke up early the next morning, still beaming. She actually got enough sleep that night, too exhausted to let the forest sounds keep her awake they way they had the night before.

Plus, today was going to be a good day, she could just feel it. They were starting off with something fun: relay races! Cassie was so excited to relax and be silly.

Cassie did her best to shower quickly. She knew a lot of people had to get ready and she didn't want to take too much time. But more importantly, she didn't want to spend too much time in the shower stall. It was one of the grossest she'd ever seen. It was all yellowed and grimy, and she was positive that some crazy insect was going to attack her at any moment. Running, screaming from the showers in a towel was not Cassie's idea of fun.

Once she was done (and secretly sprayed her hair with her smuggled-in de-tangling spray) she decided to wear her new, scrumptious BITTEN tunic sweater, with fab sailor stripes. Along with it, of course, a pair of Levi's, and her RedHeads. It was an outfit to be grateful for. It was warm but not too warm. But, more important, it was cute!

After they'd eaten another gloppy oatmeal breakfast, Craig and the other counselors led them to the race site. It was an enormous open field with different areas devoted to different activities. She and Etoile tried to figure out what games they might play. Etoile was super-excited, dancing around and squealing over the course. Cassie had no idea she was a closet relayer!

"We are gonna kick some major butt today!" Etoile said, fastening her hair into a ponytail.

"Well, aren't you the obstacle course goddess?" Cassie asked, arms folded, smiling.

"I love it! I love stuff like this!"

Cassie's competitive side soared. "Well, you just better hope we're on the same team, girlie, or else you've got some real worrying to do." Cassie tried to sound all serious, like she was in a cowboy movie. She was from Texas, after all!

"Really? Is that so?" Etoile said, her eyes gleaming.

"That is SO so!"

When Craig called the group over to one side of the field, they both laughed and ran over. As they gathered, Etoile spotted Jonah and rolled her eyes. "He's going to be so annoying during the relay races," she said.

Cassie laughed. She kind of liked Jonah. He was always funny and he could be very sweet. Cassie never would have gotten through the Fash Bash without him.

Jonah walked over to them and Cassie high-fived him. "Relays ROCK!" he shouted in Etoile's face.

Etoile winced. "Nice breath," she said, and did her best to smile at him. But before she could even force the corners of her mouth up, her face went white. Seth was headed their way and the closer he got, the more white — or maybe green — Etoile got.

Cassie noticed immediately. And she was thrilled. Now she could put her plan into action to see if Etoile really liked Seth.

Cassie high-fived Seth.

"Hey, Etoile," Seth said easily.

"Oh," Etoile said, her voice shaky. "Hey, yeah. Hey," Etoile said, and sort of waved at him.

Cassie couldn't believe how ridiculous Etoile was acting! Seth and Jonah walked to the other side of the group, toward some of the other boys.

"All right, guys," Craig said. "You've been working hard. Pushing yourselves. And I'm proud of you — we all are." Craig motioned to the other counselors and Mrs. McGinty and Mr. B. They all smiled back at them, happily.

"So," Craig continued, "before we take you on your last challenge later today, we thought you deserved a chance to play hard." He stopped very dramatically then and smiled. "Let's get ready for some relay races!" He clapped and everyone followed along.

For the next hour, Cassie and Etoile ran with eggs in spoons, guided each other blindfolded through a maze of tires, and did wheelbarrow races. Everyone — including Mary Ellen — laughed and screamed the entire time.

As they waited for the next race, Etoile clapped her hands and jumped up and down a little. "This is so awesome!" she said. "I hope we get to — "

"Next up? Three-legged race!" Craig shouted.

"Whooo!" Etoile shouted. "That's exactly what I was going to say. I love three-legged races!" She jumped up and down again and did a silly butt-wiggle dance, her hair bouncing all around.

Craig passed out pieces of twine so teammates could tie their legs together. Cassie hadn't done one of these races since Erin's tenth b'day party, back in Texas. She and Erin never won though, because they were always too busy laughing — and falling! As she turned to Etoile to ask her to be partners again, she had an idea.

A brilliant idea.

Without even thinking about the consequences, she waved Jonah and Seth over to them. Etoile was digging through her bag for an elastic and didn't realize what was going on.

"What's up, Knight?" Jonah asked.

"Let's be partners!" she said to Jonah.

"Okay, cool with me."

Just then, Etoile stood up quickly and began laughing nervously. "Ummm, Cass," she squealed, "can I talk to you for one sec?"

Seth stood there quietly. He awkwardly folded his arms.

"All right, ladies and gentlemen, we are almost ready," Mr. Blackwell shouted.

"I would love to talk, E, but we gotta go. You and Seth can race together, right? You just love these races so much, and I am so not going to be a good partner for you!"

Seth stepped forward. "You love relay races?" he asked Etoile excitedly.

Etoile turned so white, she was practically see-through. "Um, well, yeah, kind of. I mean, yeah. Right?" she stammered. She looked at Cassie, who bugged her eyes at her, which was secret code for: STOP ACTING LIKE A DORK AND CALM DOWN!

Etoile cleared her throat. "Totally," she said. "I totally love relay races." Her nervous laughter returned.

Cassie smiled. Etoile might freak out at her later but she would deal with it. Right now, Cassie was just too proud of her plan!

"Line up, guys!"

Cassie waved to Etoile — which she knew was an annoying thing to do but she couldn't resist! She and Jonah walked over to an empty spot on the starting line and quickly tied their legs together. As they did, Cassie kept her eye on Etoile and Seth. Mrs. McGinty was with them, helping them fasten the knot around their ankles.

They were all on the starting line then. Cassie looked from side to side and saw all of her class-mates, smiling and laughing — and relieved to just be acting silly. There were only two teams who were not happy. Etoile and Seth, of course, was one of them. Seth seemed happy, actually, with a toothy grin on his face, his eyes squinting over the field ahead of them, maybe developing a strategy for the race. But poor Etoile looked terrified. She just kind of stared at Seth blankly, still pale.

The other team who didn't look very happy was Mary Ellen and Lynn. Poor Lynn. It must have been really hard to be best friends with Mary Ellen. Cassie didn't know how she did it. Cassie did approve of Lynn's camp wear, though, that was for sure. Ever since her starring role in the Fash Bash, Lynn really didn't hold back her passion for fashion! Today she was wearing the cutest little maroon Adidas jacket and a pair of terry-cloth pants that Cassie had eyed in J.Crew.

Mary Ellen was practically shouting at Lynn, trying to develop a plan to win. "When they say 'go,' we should step forward with our free legs first, okay? Then move our tied legs. Start with free legs, though. Don't forget!" Mary Ellen pleaded.

Lynn nodded calmly. Cassie was impressed.

"Okay!" Craig shouted. "Racers ready?"

"READY!" the group shouted.

"On your mark!" Craig shouted.

Mr. B followed with, "Get set!"

"GO!" Mrs. McGinty screamed.

The entire group sprang to action, some teams

in perfect sync with each other, running in harmony. Other teams fell down right away, laughing and squealing as they did. Cassie and Jonah got off to a strong start, arms locked, determination pushing them forward. Cassie was trying to keep her concentration on moving her middle leg with Jonah's, but she was distracted wondering about Etoile. Was she okay? Or did Cassie push too hard to get her to talk with Seth?

But Cassie was relieved as soon as she spotted Etoile and Seth. The two were sailing forward together up ahead of them, laughing like old friends. Hooray! Cassie knew E could have fun with Seth!

Nearly forgetting she was in the race too, Cassie felt something pulling her down to the ground. While she was focusing on Etoile, she'd fallen out of sync with Jonah and before she could do anything to fix it, he'd lost his footing and stumbled. Cassie locked her arm tighter with his and tried to regain their composure. She shouted, "Left foot! Right foot! Left foot! Right foot! Left! Right!" just like Craig had done on the raft.

In a matter of seconds, they found their pace again and she and Jonah hobbled forward, passing a few teams along with way. "Left! Right! Left! Right!" Cassie yelled.

"You're awesome, Knight!" Jonah yelled.

Cassie smiled. She was actually helping her team to do well. She was being sporty! And loving it!

She could see the finish line up ahead and heard the screams of her fellow classmates around her. Cassie threw her feet forward, pushing herself as hard as she could. Mary Ellen and Lynn were in the lead but there were some teams close on their heels, including Etoile and Seth!

They ran forward, Jonah yelling now, "Right! Left!" and Cassie doing her best to keep them moving in a straight line. Cassie heard shouting ahead and saw that Mary Ellen and Lynn had just crossed the finish line, coming in first.

Something came over Cassie then. She wanted second place. She surveyed the field and saw that Etoile and Seth, their only major competition, had toppled over in a flailing heap of laughter. Cassie pulled Jonah's arm tight and shouted, "Let's do this!"

Together, they raced forward, passing a few struggling teams, then the giggling heap on the ground that was Etoile and Seth, and finally — finally — over the finish line! They made it! Second place was theirs!

They both fell to the ground, ecstatic. Jonah untied their legs. They jumped up together and hugged, and Mrs. McGinty came running over to give them a red second-place ribbon. "Second place!" Mrs. McGinty shouted. "Cassie and Jonah!"

Seth and Etoile had recovered themselves and were right on their heels, toppling onto the finish line in third place. Cassie was so excited for all of them. She looked over and saw Seth handing the yellow ribbon to Etoile, insisting that she keep it.

Beaming — and hugging everyone she could get her hands on — Cassie caught her breath. Mrs. McGinty came over and hugged Cassie. "Hey, you! Second place! Congratulations!"

"Thanks!" Cassie gasped.

Mary Ellen walked over then. "Isn't it great, Mary Ellen?" her mother asked her.

"Sure!" Mary Ellen said, an evil smile on her face. "Too bad second place is first worst, though." She held her blue ribbon out to Cassie and stormed away.

"Mary Ellen!" Mrs. McGinty shouted. "I'm sorry, Cassie. Please excuse her." And with that, Mrs. McGinty followed Mary Ellen.

"She is such a nerd," Jonah said, rolling his eyes.

Cassie didn't know why it mattered anymore, but Mary Ellen's cruelty still really upset her. She tried to push it out of her mind, but she just felt sad. Cassie wanted to walk away from the group, before they could see that she was hurt. She didn't want to ruin anyone's fun.

Just then, Etoile and Seth walked over. Seth and Jonah immediately started to compare notes about the race. Etoile ran to Cassie and hugged her but knew something was wrong immediately.

"What happened?" Etoile asked.

"Mary Ellen just made me feel bad. Again," Cassie said, a tear dropping from her eye.

"Oh, Cass. I'm so sorry. But you can't let her get to you, okay?"

"I know," Cassie said. And she did know. In her head. But it was hard to tell her heart the same thing.

"Well, there's no time for being sad right now because the final event is gonna start," Etoile said, smiling. "And you have to be my teammate."

Cassie wiped her eyes. "I do?"

"I'm serious," Etoile said. "I can't do the final event without the girl who beat me!"

"I did beat you, didn't I?" Cassie asked, smiling. Etoile could always make her feel better.

"Yeah, you did! That's why I need you on my team!"

She threw her arm around Cassie and walked her to the next setup.

"What's next, anyway?" Cassie asked.

Etoile pointed across the field, and Cassie's jaw dropped. An obstacle course, complete with tires to run through, logs to balance on — and a wall to scale at the end!

"You've *got* to be kidding me," Cassie said.

"I wish I was!" Etoile said. "But you have no choice, missy! It's a partner race. And I plan to win."

"Fine, then me and Seth will be a team. We are gonna whup you!" Jonah said. Seth laughed and shrugged his shoulders.

"Oh, no you're not," Etoile said. She grabbed Cassie's hand, and they all laughed and ran ahead.

CHAPTER 10

Cassie Knight, Queen of the Jungle?

Cassie and Etoile didn't even come close to winning the obstacle course. Naturally, Mary Ellen and Lynn came in first. Cassie almost congratulated Mary Ellen but stopped herself before she did. She thought it might be best to just leave her alone for a while.

After they ate lunch, the group headed to the final activity, one that made Cassie feel nauseated.

A bungee jump.

There was something about heights that Cassie couldn't deal with. Back in their old house in Houston, they had a little walkway over their living room and Cassie didn't even like walking on that. She always felt so wonky up there. As they neared the jump site, Cassie grew more and more quiet as her nerves grew inside her.

"You know that like a million people have done this before, right?" Etoile asked.

"I know. I know. But that doesn't matter at all," Cassie said, trying to breathe normally. "*I've* never done it!"

"Nothing bad is going to happen. I promise." Etoile said.

"Uh-huh." Cassie was not convinced.

When they arrived at the bungee, Cassie's stomach flipped. She looked up and up and up to the very top and felt sick. It was so high in the sky! And even worse, they had to climb up a crazy, skinny metal ladder to the top, where there was only a tiny ledge for them to stand on before they jumped. People started to whisper to one another when they saw it. But not Cassie. She felt even less like talking now that she was actually seeing what she was going to have to do!

"I know this looks really scary," Mr. Blackwell said to the group. "But I promise you, it is completely safe. And really fun. This is one of the reasons I wanted to come on this trip. I love bungee jumping and you will, too, once you do it."

"And Mr. Blackwell has volunteered to go first," Craig said.

"Okay, here I go!" Mr. B said, and headed to the long ladder up to the top, where Meghan, the counselor, was standing in place to help him.

Craig spoke as Mr. B climbed the ladder. "Okay, guys. Now, Mr. Blackwell is climbing the ladder very carefully. One foot at a time, no rush."

They all watched as he went from rung to rung, growing smaller and smaller in the sky.

"Once he reaches the top, we'll help him get the harness on." Craig bent down and grabbed a harness that was next to him. "It's easy to put on and will stay securely on you with these four latches," he said, pointing to the metal clasps.

"And once you're secured, we'll count to three. And on three, you just step forward. No need to jump or run. Just take an easy step forward."

Easy step forward? Cassie thought. *That's going to be the hardest step I'll ever take!*

Craig had a megaphone in his hand. He held it up to his mouth. "Okay, you ready up there?" Mr. Blackwell looked down and gave the thumbs-up.

"All right, then, good luck!" Craig shouted through the megaphone, his voice echoing out into the open sky.

They all looked up and watched. They faintly heard "One — two — three!" and watched as Mr. B stepped forward off the platform and zoomed down toward the ground. He let out one yelp and then he smiled super-big. He bounced down on the bungee, flew back up, and let out a giant "Whoo-hoo!"

And not even a minute later, he was back with the group, flushed and happy. "It was awesome!" he said to everyone. "You are going to love it! It's so beautiful up there!"

Everyone formed a line, and one at a time they went up the ladder, got into the harness, and jumped. Cassie couldn't believe it. How could anyone think this was fun? Her heart pounded as she watched each person, one by one, make the long climb and jump. People seemed to be enjoying it, though, even the ones who hesitated a little. Seth took a moment before he jumped and when he did he screamed like Tarzan the entire time. He made everyone laugh, even Mary Ellen. Jonah really took his time before he jumped and when he did, he squealed at the top of his lungs from beginning to end, while Seth shouted encouragement into the megaphone: "Jo-nah! Jo-nah!"

Cassie was happy she was right behind Etoile,

because her friend handled the whole thing like a pro. Of course. Etoile climbed the ladder deliberately, listened attentively to the counselor at the top as she got into the harness, adjusted the elastic in her hair, and then jumped gracefully, flying through the air. She looked happy, terrified, and thrilled all at the same time.

The moment Etoile landed, Cassie ran to her and gave her a giant hug. She was so proud of Etoile!

"It's awesome!" Etoile yelled.

This felt like the exact opposite of awesome for Cassie. She didn't even like to jump off the low diving board at the swimming pool. As she climbed the ladder, she tried to think of the right word for what this was. Un-awesome? Non-awesome? Anti-awesome?

She'd made her way to the top before she could decide on the word.

"Hey, Cassie!" Meghan said cheerily when Cassie reached the top.

"Meghan," Cassie cleared her throat, "do I really have to do this?"

Meghan must have been used to this type of panicky question because she still went about her job, helping Cassie into the harness. "You don't have to do it but you should. It really is fun. I promise you."

Cassie tried to swallow but her throat was dry. "Is it normal that my throat is dry? Maybe that's not a good thing and I shouldn't . . ."

Meghan leaned forward and grabbed a water bottle from a little ledge. "Want a sip?"

Before she could answer, Meghan was spraying water into Cassie's mouth. Then Meghan put her hands on Cassie's shoulders. "Okay, Cassie, this is it. Nice and easy. You're all ready. Just turn. And at the count of three, you just step off the platform."

"Umm, well, I . . ." Cassie was speechless.

Meghan turned her around and took a step back. "Okay, Cassie, here I go."

Cassie's heart pounded hard.

"One!"

She closed her eyes and put her head down.

"Two!"

Cassie made a big mistake then and opened her eyes. She saw everyone beneath her, staring up. She began to panic, her hands sweating and her heart pounding in her ears.

"Three!"

Cassie closed her eyes.

And nothing happened. She just couldn't take that step forward.

She felt the breeze on her face and the warm sun. It was very quiet.

"Are you okay?" Meghan finally said, behind her.

"I'm fine," Cassie lied.

"Want me to count again?"

"Sure."

"One . . . two . . . three!"

And still, nothing. Cassie just couldn't. If she closed her eyes, she felt queasy. And if she kept them open, well, she was just terrified by the view!

"Do you want to skip this activity, Cassie?" Meghan asked gently. "You can if you want to."

Just then, Etoile called up to Cassie on the megaphone. Other people that jumped before her had gotten calls of encouragement from their friends and it totally helped them to jump. But nothing was going to get her to do this.

"C'mon, Cass! You can do this!" Etoile called out.

Cassie looked down, trying not to panic. Her feet were glued to the platform. She put her hand on the glittery carabiner that Erin had sent her, try-ing to absorb some of its positive energy. She just didn't think she'd be able to move them, no matter how hard she tried.

She squeezed her eyes closed. If she didn't want to do it, she didn't have to. But she would have to walk down — and forever be the person who didn't do the jump. That didn't feel so great. She could push herself to do all of those other things — she could brave any river, climb any mountain. But not this.

Suddenly, Cassie heard a new voice over the megaphone. "Cassie Cyan Knight! You are one of the bravest people I have ever met. Now, stop your fussing and jump!"

Cassie slowly opened her eyes and looked down again. Mary Ellen was standing at the front of the crowd below, holding the megaphone to her mouth.

"I am going to count to three. And you let go at three, okay?" Mary Ellen yelled.

Cassie took a deep breath. She nodded yes.

"ONE!" Mary Ellen shouted.

Cassie took another deep breath.

"TWO!"

Cassie relaxed her quaking legs as much as she could.

"THA-REE!" Mary Ellen shouted in a perfectly encouraging voice.

Cassie didn't know what it was, but Mary Ellen's voice felt so real and so believable, that without any hesitation, she simply . . .

JUMPED!

In an instant, she was flying through the air! When she managed to open her eyes, all she saw was lovely, blue sky with marshmallow clouds and then, looking down, the green, green grass beneath her. She was screaming, but it was a scream of total, utter excitement and happiness. She saw the rest of the group staring up at her. Etoile was jumping up and down, clapping her hands.

"Waaaaa-hoooooo!!" Cassie yelled, the wind in her hair.

As she neared the ground, she sprung right back up again, this time at a slower speed. She imagined that she was Supergirl, flying from the top of a building, justice on her side and a gorgeous crimson cape flowing around her. She looked down again and saw everyone cheering her on — including Mary Ellen. Cassie couldn't believe it, but there she was, shouting and clapping like crazy.

Cassie's smiled widened as she sank closer to the ground. This time, when she bounced down again, the counselors grabbed the bungee and pulled Cassie over to a ledge. They helped her out of her harness and as soon as she was free, she ran down the steps, headed for Etoile.

But before she could even realize what was happening, Mary Ellen came running at her fast, her hair falling out of her scrunchy, flying wildly. When she got nearer to Cassie, she opened her arms wide.

Cassie was shocked! What was she supposed to do? Run into her arms and give her a big hug?

Mary Ellen?

Really?

But there was no time to decide and before she knew it, Mary Ellen was clutching Cassie, hugging her.

"I never thought you were going to do it!" she shouted in Cassie's ear.

Cassie jumped up and down with Mary Ellen, still slightly confused. But she couldn't resist being happy. She did it. She jumped. And mean Mary Ellen had helped her to do it!

Life Rule #77: Happiness. Go with it.

This was just too amazing and awesome of a moment to question, so Cassie went with it.

"It was so incredible!" she shouted back at Mary Ellen.

The two girls continued jumping up and down, wildly excited and then they realized something: Everyone was watching them!

It didn't matter to Cassie at all. She was so grateful to Mary Ellen and happy to show the entire class.

But Mary Ellen pulled away from the hug and her face went grim; it was the Mary Ellen face Cassie was used to.

"Yes, that was great," Mary Ellen grumbled then, crossing her arms.

Not sure what to do, Cassie stared blankly, searching for something to say.

Before she could come up with anything, Etoile jumped in front of Cassie and threw her arms around her.

"You are the goddess of the air!" she shouted.

Cassie hugged Etoile back, still breathless, and watched as Mary Ellen walked away from the crowd.

In a matter of seconds, everyone was huddled around Cassie to congratulate her, but somehow, Cassie couldn't take her mind off of Mary Ellen.

CHAPTER 11

Girls Just Wanna

The rest of the day was spent with a final natural classroom session, where they learned all about the trees of Maine. Cassie had no idea there were so many different kinds of pine trees. She was also surprised to find out that Maine's state flower was the white pinecone. As she listened to Meghan and Craig, she reached over and picked a cluster of three baby pinecones. They were so pretty, with all of their deep ridges and tiny stems. Cassie thought there was something so perfect about them, so she stashed them in her little backpack.

Back at the campground, they were told to freshen up before dinner and the final night party. Cassie wondered what was going to happen there. Mary Ellen talked about it a lot, and Cassie hoped it was something really fun. *It* better *be fun,* she thought, as she changed into a pair of Levi's skinny jeans and her peekaboo pumps, which she had kept a secret, even to Etoile.

"I can't believe you brought those!" Etoile squealed when she saw Cassie take them out of the bottom of her big backpack.

"I know. I couldn't resist. Don't be mad, okay?" she asked Etoile. They had promised each other they wouldn't bring anything extra to wear.

"I won't be mad about those, if you don't get about this," Etoile said, pulling an *E* original out of her backpack. It was the cutest jean skirt, covered with tons of plaid patches.

Cassie's jaw dropped. "Did you make that?"

"No. Well, sorta — I just sewed all the patches on."

"It's beautiful!"

Etoile looked at the skirt and grinned. "Thanks! I love it!"

As they did final looks in their tiny compact mirrors, Cassie grabbed her carabiner and fastened it to her belt loop.

Finally ready, Cassie and Etoile walked over to the picnic tables to meet up with everyone. They sat with Deirdre and Margery for the feast of campfire-roasted hot dogs and beans. Cassie was a little grossed out when she saw the cans of beans being opened up and dumped into a big pot. But to her surprise, it was one of the most delicious meals she'd eaten since arriving at The Gamut.

While they ate, they compared notes about their bungee experiences. Margery was always on top of the cheerleading pyramid, so Cassie was convinced she would have been okay with the jump, but she wasn't.

"I was petrified!" she gasped. "I swear, if it wasn't for you, Cassie, I wouldn't have been able to do it."

"That is so sweet of you, Margery!"

"Mary Ellen really helped you, huh?" Deirdre asked.

Cassie didn't even know how to answer. She didn't want to tell Deirdre how hurt she was, so she settled on, "Yeah, she did." Cassie looked over at Mary Ellen, who was sitting with her mom and Mr. B, talking about the final plans for the party, Cassie was sure.

"Okay, guys," Craig said, standing. "When you're finished, everyone should head over to the fire and pick up some s'mores. You can eat them on your way down to the Main House for our final night party."

Yum! S'mores were definitely one of Cassie's favorites and eating them hot off the fire made them even more perfect.

As they munched, Cassie and Etoile followed the group to the Main House. This time around, they were allowed take a smooth path that was normally reserved for staff. It was lit by small, yellow lights. Cassie was glad to not have to deal with the perils of crossing the water once more, especially in her pumps!

"Hello, they could have let us walk this path on the way here!" Etoile said.

Cassie thought back to her big, silly fall in the water and laughed.

"What?" Etoile said.

"Nothing. I just kind of can't believe the trip is almost over."

"I know," Etoile said.

"I really had fun, E. I mean it was so hard — like today was the hardest thing I've ever done. And I totally did it!" Cassie said, beaming.

"The hardest thing you've ever done? C'mon!" Etoile said, pulling her ponytail tighter. "You moved to Maine from Texas, and you were a total rock star about it. *That* was hard."

Cassie looked at Etoile as they walked. "That *was* sort of hard," she said.

Cassie wondered what Erin and the girls back in Texas were up to. She couldn't wait to go back to civilization and talk to all of them! They would never believe what she'd accomplished in just a few days.

"Of course moving was hard!" Etoile said. "And you made it look easy. I know this camp stuff was tough for you, but I knew you could do it." Etoile was still fixing her ponytail.

"Thanks. I knew you could do it, too!"

"I kind of loved all of it," Etoile said, finally done with her hair.

"AND you talked to Seth Gordon," Cassie whispered.

Etoile blushed. "Oh, right! I should be very mad at you! I cannot believe you made me do the race with him!" Etoile gave Cassie a playful slap on the arm.

"You were being so ridiculous about it. You can talk to anybody. There was no reason not to talk to him."

"Well," Etoile said. "You're right." She smiled sheepishly. "He is really nice."

"And cute, too?" Cassie asked, raising her eyebrows.

Etoile blushed. "Stop!" she said. And then, changing the subject brilliantly, she said, "And I think we were enormously successful at reinventing camp wear!"

Cassie could always be distracted by fashion. She did a quick twirl in her final-night's outfit.

Etoile did the same, her pleated jean skirt flaring out.

"We are a success story!" Cassie said, smiling.

As they walked, Cassie looked at their fellow campers, everyone walking in a big group together. They all looked so happy to be there.

Mary Ellen was walking with Lynn ahead of them. Cassie was trying not to feel upset about how Mary Ellen had run away from her earlier. But Cassie *was* upset. It seemed silly for Mary Ellen to always be so hard on Cassie. There was no reason for it.

When they finally reached the Main House, the campers were excited to see a big banner hanging over the front that read CONGRATULATIONS CAMPERS! It felt so exciting to be at the end of the trip and to realize how much they all had accomplished.

Craig led them all inside. The room was lit with candles and there was a big table of snacks and soda set out for them. After they settled into comfy chairs and couches, Craig announced that it was tradition to end the last night with awards — and of course, some fun.

"On behalf of all the counselors here, I want to tell you how great you all are. You were brave. You were focused. And you learned a bit about the rich Maine landscape — and yourselves, too." He clapped and everyone joined him.

"These are a hard few days. We know that. And to show you how proud we are of all of you, we have some awards to give out."

Mr. Blackwell appeared through the doorway then, rolling a cart of trophies.

Mrs. McGinty stood up and joined him and Craig at the front of the group.

"Guys," Mr. B said. "You did it. And that is so cool."

Mrs. McGinty laughed. "And I did it, too! I can't believe that!"

Cassie hadn't realized that the activities they did might be hard for Mr. B or Mrs. McGinty. And as they started handing out awards, Cassie watched in sheer delight as her friends got noticed for all of their hard work.

She beamed when Etoile and Seth won the team-work award for the three-legged race. And when Lynn won the sportsmanship award, Cassie gave her a standing ovation. Jonah even won the most humorous award and did a cartwheel on his way up to the podium!

"The award for 'Good Spirit' is always a tough one," Craig said, holding the little pine tree trophy in his hand. "So many of you could win it. But all of the counselors agreed that one person was truly the most deserving." He paused for a moment. "And that person is Cassie Knight," Craig said, smiling.

But Cassie wasn't expecting to hear her own name called. Jonah gave her a little nudge and Cassie realized that everyone was waiting for her to go up and get it. She blushed for a moment but by the time she was shaking Craig's hand, she was so happy that she even did a little jump. It made some people laugh. Margery called out, "Go, Cassie!"

Cassie sat back down and showed the award to Etoile, who put her arm around Cassie. "Congratulations! You so deserve that!"

Craig spoke again. "The final award goes to the camper that we think did the most they could to make this a positive experience for everyone around them. And we are very proud to give it to . . ." He paused again. "None other than Mary Ellen McGinty!"

Mrs. McGinty and Mr. B started to clap and Mary Ellen stood up. Cassie could tell that she was totally surprised, because Mary Ellen's face was so happy — and shocked — there was no way she could have been acting.

Everyone applauded and cheered. But Cassie couldn't help but wonder if Mary Ellen really should have won the award. She always seemed so tough and negative with everyone. She was hard on Lynn and the other campers, always bossing people around. And not to mention how hard she was on Cassie about what to pack, how to hike, when not to laugh . . . All of it just seemed so mean! And then running away after their hug? Cassie just didn't get it.

Mary Ellen walked to the front of the room, and her mom gave her a big hug. She accepted the award very politely and sat down.

"Okay, guys, now that we've all been rewarded, we thought we could have some fun!" Craig said happily. "Mrs. McGinty and Mary Ellen have prepared some terrific games for all of us. So let's take a five-minute break while they get set up."

People applauded.

Etoile and Cassie headed toward the snack table. There were more s'mores there and they couldn't get enough of them!

Standing with Etoile, crunching away, Cassie wondered out loud why Mary Ellen won her award.

"Well," Etoile said, thinking hard, her eyes squinting behind her glasses. "Yes. I think she deserved it."

"Really? But she can be so mean!" Cassie said.

"She can be mean. I know. But she's always kind of watching out for people in her own weird way. Like, she wants people to do everything right. And that's kind of annoying, but there's nothing really wrong with that," Etoile said.

Cassie rolled her eyes. She'd never thought of it that way. Sometimes she didn't want Etoile to be so smart! Maybe she was right, though.

"And, wait, HELLO!" Etoile said so quickly that Cassie could almost see the lightbulb above her head. "She got you to do the bungee jump! I mean, that was something very special!"

Cassie couldn't disagree with Etoile. Mary Ellen did help Cassie to take that jump. And to not bring magazines on the trip. And she did help other people, too. Cassie looked over at Mary Ellen. Lynn and Deirdre and some other people were all standing with her, congratulating her on her award. And even though Mary Ellen was being kind and polite, she was working hard to set up the next activities. Some people asked if they could help, but Mary Ellen said no. She even made Lynn and Deirdre sit down so they could enjoy their s'mores. It seemed like everyone really admired Mary Ellen and understood her. Maybe it was time for Cassie to do the same.

Feeling inspired, Cassie decided to congratulate Mary Ellen. "I'll be right back," she said to Etoile, and approached Mary Ellen, who was busy separating slips of paper into piles.

"Are we playing charades?" Cassie asked, trying to sound casual.

Mary Ellen looked up, surprised. "Yes. We are." She went back to the slips of paper.

"I love charades!" Cassie said.

"Good. I'm glad," Mary Ellen said matter-of-factly.

Cassie wanted to walk away and give up on Mary Ellen once and for all, but she stopped herself and planted her feet firmly on the ground.

"I didn't mean to disturb you while you were setting up. I just wanted to congratulate you on your award. You deserve it," Cassie said, and began to walk away.

"They had to give it to me," Mary Ellen said, her face looking very serious.

"Huh?" Cassie asked. She was so taken by surprise that it was all she could think to say.

"They did. I mean, I was peer leader. My mother was parent coordinator. What else were they going to do?" Mary Ellen went back to sorting.

Mary Ellen was just as hard on herself as she was with other people. "No. That's not true," Cassie said quietly.

"Of course it is. My mother is here, they had to do it." Mary Ellen sounded so defeated.

"No, they didn't. They gave it to you because you were awesome on this trip and because you helped so many people to do their best."

Mary Ellen stood up then, to face Cassie. "Really? Do you mean that?" she asked.

"Yes, I mean that! I don't really lie, if you haven't noticed," Cassie said.

"I've noticed," Mary Ellen said, giving Cassie a look.

"So then believe me, okay? You made this trip the best it could possibly be. You challenged us by making us learn about totally icky things. And you got me to bungee jump! That is not an easy thing, you know. I am petrified of heights."

Mary Ellen smiled as Cassie spoke. "Really?"

"Umm, more than really! Totally!"

Mrs. McGinty came over then and put her arm around Mary Ellen. "How are we doing? Almost ready to start playing?"

"We're ready," Mary Ellen said.

"Well, let's get started."

Mary Ellen smiled at Cassie. "Thank you," she said kindly.

"Thank you!" Cassie said back, and she started to walk back to Etoile and some of the others.

"Cassie?" Mary Ellen called.

Cassie turned. "You know you weren't supposed to bring those shoes, right?"

Cassie frowned. Was Mary Ellen being serious?

But then, Mary Ellen winked and began laughing. Cassie laughed, too, happy that she'd spoken with Mary Ellen.

Charades started out with a bang. Cassie could feel excitement in the air. Everyone seemed glad to just have time for fun. The past few days had been demanding and it was nice to relax. People shouted and giggled as they played. Even Mr. B was playing and laughing along with his team. Everyone was able to guess Cassie's clues — except one. She had no idea how to show "Magic Mountain" with hand motions!

But as the game went on, people seemed to be

less interested. They weren't nearly as eager to play their turns. Some people were even yawning.

Uh-oh, Cassie thought. *This is not a good way for this night to end.*

She looked around the room nervously, not wanting Mary Ellen's game to fail. As she looked, her eyes locked with Mary Ellen's. Cassie could tell that Mary Ellen was thinking the same thing.

Mary Ellen stood up and sneaked over to Cassie and Etoile.

"This is a complete disaster," she whispered. "I may be good at some things, but I am not good with stuff like this."

"What do you mean?" Cassie asked.

Mary Ellen spun her eyes around at the room, annoyed.

"No, it's fine! People are having fun," Cassie said, trying to sound convincing.

Mary Ellen stood up then and pulled Cassie and Etoile in to the corner. No one seemed to even notice.

"No. They *were* having fun. Now they're not." She stopped then and Cassie thought she saw tears in her eyes. "I just don't want people to remember this as the end of their adventure," she said then.

Mary Ellen was looking for help. Cassie couldn't believe it. And neither could Etoile, who stood there with her mouth open, shocked.

"Okay, well, what's the next activity?" Etoile asked.

"There isn't one," Mary Ellen said, panicked. "I thought charades would be enough."

Cassie's eyes grew big.

The three girls looked over at the campers, who were lazily playing now. Some people were actually falling asleep. And it was only seven o'clock!

"Maybe we could do, like, an art project?" Etoile said.

Before Cassie could try to let Etoile down easy, Mary Ellen snapped, "We can't do something like that! Like the boys are going to want to do a craft?"

Etoile pulled her head back in shock slightly.

"E, we just need to make sure it's something that would be fun for everyone, you know?"

"I know," Etoile said calmly.

"And you owe me that knitting lesson still, you know?!" Cassie said.

Etoile smiled. "Right! I can't wait to show you a new —"

"Okay, ladies," Mary Ellen interrupted, "we need an idea for now. For all of these people. Let's stay focused."

Cassie and Etoile turned their heads to glare at Mary Ellen and then the three of them laughed.

"Okay, I get it!" Mary Ellen said. "Sorry."

Right then, as if a swirl of pixie dust blew over her, Cassie had a brilliant idea.

"Hold on!" she squealed. She grabbed her backpack and dug through it. She found her lip gloss and gave her lips a quick Honeypot application.

"Lip gloss? What are we going to do with lip gloss?" Mary Ellen asked.

Cassie held her finger up to say "wait" as she finished application.

"She doesn't like to be disturbed during her glossing," Etoile said, half kidding. "It's very complicated."

Mary Ellen snorted, which made all three of them laugh again.

When she was done, Cassie tossed the gloss into her bag and dug around for another moment. Then she pulled out her nano.

"What? We're all going to take turns listening to one earphone or something?" Mary Ellen, asked, again not realizing how mean she was being!

"Oh, no," Cassie said coyly, proud of her idea. "This is something much better." She held her teal nano out and changed the course of the entire evening with one word:

"Nano-oke!"

The three girls looked at one another, thrilled. "Everyone loves karaoke! And there's like a zillion songs they can choose from on here."

"You're a genius, Cassie, you really are," Mary Ellen said before dashing off to find her mother and Craig. All they needed was to plug into the sound system and they would be in business!

"Wait, wait, wait," Cassie said, grabbing Mary Ellen's arm before she got away. "We have to do the first number, girls," Cassie said.

"No way," Etoile said.

Cassie looked at Mary Ellen intently. She had to say yes after everything they'd been through, helping each other this week.

Mary Ellen swallowed hard. "You have 'Girls Just Want to Have Fun'?" she asked Cassie, suddenly very serious.

Cassie was shocked all over again. "I mean, yeah! Of course I do!" she cried. It was one of her absolute favorite songs. She and her mom sang it together constantly.

"My mom loves that song," Mary Ellen said. "She's been singing it to me forever."

"Mine too!" both Cassie and Etoile said. Cassie looked at Etoile in amazement. She didn't know that very important fact about her bestie!

Beaming now, Cassie said, "Okay, girls, are we ready to have some fun? Let's get everyone super-excited!"

Mary Ellen's face looked more serious than when she took a math test. "Let's do this," she said, squinting. "Give me one minute to tell my mom and Craig." Mary Ellen darted off, with Cassie's nano in her hand.

A moment later, Mary Ellen returned. "Okay, they're going to hook it up and we're up first!"

It was all happening so fast. And Cassie knew she had some serious styling to do before they were introduced. She grabbed both girls and pulled them into the Ladies'. "Hair and makeup check," she shouted.

Once inside the minty-green bathroom, Cassie opened her backpack and took out the few things she had with her that would be of any assistance. Gloss. Brush. Elastics.

Etoile looked in her purse and produced the same. She had her Sugar Icing gloss with her. The pink was perfect for Mary Ellen's complexion.

"Mary Ellen, you should try this gloss," Etoile said.

"What?" Mary Ellen said, standing there, slightly confused. "No, thank you. I don't wear stuff like that."

"Yeah, but you're going to be onstage," Cassie said, putting her hand on her hip.

Etoile held the gloss tube up to her. "You just squeeze a little bit out and apply it. It's simple."

Mary Ellen took the tube and did as she was told. She swiped the gloss across her lips and instantly, she looked completely glam. She got close to the mirror to see herself.

"Wow," she said excitedly, "is it supposed to be sparkly?"

"Yes! That's the whole point," Cassie said seriously.

"Wow," Mary Ellen said again, moving her head around a little so the light would catch the glittery gloss.

Cassie knew there was only one thing left to do for Mary Ellen. Hair.

Cassie turned to the mirror and fluffed her own curls a bit. They were in serious need of a good conditioning treatment after all they'd been through on this trip. She pulled out her Pro-V spray and spritzed the shine back into her hair.

As she did, Etoile took her hair down and began brushing her own straight locks. They magically got smoother and shinier. Etoile had great hair.

"You know, you're lucky the mosquitoes didn't attack you with all that stuff in your hair," Mary Ellen said.

Cassie rolled her eyes but was secretly relieved that she didn't have to deal with that, too.

"Okay, now, hair for you," Cassie said, looking at Mary Ellen's blond hair. "Etoile's going to brush it first."

Etoile nodded and stepped behind Mary Ellen. She pulled Mary Ellen's tartan scrunchy off and went to work.

Mary Ellen was quiet, still dazzled by the glitter of the gloss.

Etoile began to brush the back of Mary Ellen's hair and in a moment, her blond frizzy flyaways were tame and shiny, smoother than they'd ever been.

"Whoa," Mary Ellen said when Etoile was finished.

Cassie clapped her hands. "You are SO going to be Etoile's model on *Project Runway*!" Cassie gave some Pro-V sprays to Mary Ellen's hair.

Mary Ellen blushed. "Should I put my scrunchy back on?"

"Not with that hair you shouldn't!" Cassie said.

"Really?"

"Yes!" Etoile said adamantly. "It's awesome!"

"But wait!" Cassie said, digging though her bag. She pulled out the pinecones she'd picked up earlier. "How about these?"

"In my hair?" Mary Ellen asked, twisting her face.

"Yes!" Etoile and Cassie shouted together.

In a moment, they had managed to work the three baby pinecones into the elastic that held Mary Ellen's hair back. It was super-natural-chic!

Mary Ellen turned her head so she could see her hair in the mirror. "Wow, it's so nice!" she said happily.

Cassie fluffed her curls a bit and wished she had something cute to hold it back.

"You don't happen to have . . ." Cassie stopped herself.

"What?" Mary Ellen asked, her eyes wide.

"I would love a headband to hold my hair back, and I thought maybe you might have one?"

"Of course!" Mary Ellen ran to her backpack and pulled out a pretty green satin band. "How's this?" she asked, handing it to Cassie.

Cassie took the headband from Mary Ellen and put it on her head. It immediately gave her a new look and she was excited. The camper-chic thing was a hard one to maintain. She stepped back and checked her outfit in the mirror.

Mrs. McGinty poked her head into the bathroom. "Girls! The music is all set up. We're ready for you!"

Cassie and Etoile leaned in to the mirror to apply a last swipe of lip gloss. Mary Ellen gave herself a very serious look-over in the mirror, between them.

"You look good, girl!" Cassie said.

Mary Ellen smiled. "Thanks. A lot!"

They all did an about-face and walked toward the main room. Mrs. McGinty's face lit up when she saw Mary Ellen.

"Honey, look at you!" she said.

Mary Ellen smiled at her mom. "I look okay, right?"

"You look fabulous!" Mrs. McGinty exclaimed. She wrapped her arms around Mary Ellen. She composed herself after a moment and then stepped back. "Okay, girls, you all look wonderful. Get out there and have some fun!" She held her hand up to Craig, so he would start the music.

Suddenly, the bubbly music flowed from the speakers, through the Main House, even out of the speakers on the campgrounds outside.

Nervousness swirled through Cassie's stomach. Etoile was almost green. But Mary Ellen was focused, calm, and ready.

When they heard the music, the other campers looked around, confused.

The three girls ran to the front of the room and grabbed the microphones.

"All right, campers!" Mary Ellen shouted. "It's time for a little fun. Thanks to my friends Cassie and Etoile . . . we present to you . . . NANO-OKE!"

The crowd was silent, slightly stunned to see Mary Ellen being so relaxed — not to mention wearing lip gloss and a new hairstyle.

The music cue hit perfectly then. Cassie had to compose herself. Mary Ellen said they were friends!

But there was no time for drama. Cassie had to sing. She started singing the song's opening lines, and the girls joined in.

People began to hoot and holler immediately as they sang and danced around on the stage. Cassie was pretty sure they didn't sound anywhere near perfect but they were having a lot of fun. They even took turns taking solos.

Mary Ellen wailed her part and the crowd applauded the whole way through.

Feeling especially brave and proud, Cassie led the girls out into the middle of the audience and the three of them sang together,

Girls — they want to have fun

Oh, girls just want to have fun.

Cassie, Etoile, and Mary Ellen sang their hearts out and felt like the dreamiest Dreamgirls ever! Before they ended, Cassie led the group back onto the stage and they ended with their arms up in the air.

The audience roared and the three girls took their bows, radiant and exhilarated.

"Total success!" Etoile said.

"Awesome!" Cassie seconded.

Mary Ellen turned to face them. "You guys are brilliant. Thank you so much!" She put her arms out to Etoile and gave her a big hug. Then she turned to Cassie and when they hugged, Mary Ellen said, "I don't know what we ever did without you here, Cassie."

Before she could respond, Lynn came running onto the stage to hug Mary Ellen. Cassie watched as the two friends jumped up and down together, Mary Ellen acting like someone Cassie could really be friends with. As she looked out at the room, Cassie couldn't believe her eyes, everyone was lined up to sing. Jonah and Seth were even planning to do a Jonas Brothers' song.

"You saved this party, you know?" Mary Ellen said to Cassie as they stepped off the little stage.

"No, I didn't."

"You did! Are you kidding me?" Mary Ellen asked incredulously.

"I didn't save it. WE did. Together."

"I guess we did," she responded.

"Well, us and a little lip gloss," Cassie said.

Etoile put her arms around both of them. "We just wanna! We just wanna!" she sang.

The three girls laughed and started to whisper about what song they should sing next.

CHAPTER 12

Time to Go

No one could believe it, but the last morning was finally here. They ate their oatmeal — Cassie was so relieved it was her last morning of it — and headed to their tents to pack up the last of their things. Everyone was kind of quiet, thinking about all of the incredible things they had done at The Gamut.

When they were all ready, they loaded onto the bus, each camper giving Craig and the counselors big hugs before they did. Cassie was sad to be leaving. The Gamut may have beaten her up a few times, but she felt like a totally different person now. She could bungee jump and hike and be near worms and so much more! Cassie Cyan Knight never thought she would be able to say those things about herself.

Life Rule #17: You never know!

She and Etoile sat right behind Mary Ellen and Lynn in the front of the bus. The four girls had talked most of the night before and even stayed up past curfew together.

"Want me to sit by the window?" Etoile asked, knowing Cassie hated her hair being blown around.

Cassie was about to say yes, her automatic response, and then changed her mind. "Would you mind if I did?" She wanted to get some last looks at the beautiful campgrounds and woods.

"Not at all," Etoile said, stepping out of Cassie's way.

As they settled in, Jonah and Seth walked past them. Cassie said "hi" to both of them, and as Seth said hi to Etoile, he tripped and stumbled forward nervously.

He recovered quickly, though. "Hi," he said, smiling. Jonah started laughing, and poor Seth turned a perfect shade of crimson.

"C'mon, Gordon, keep it moving!" Jonah said, rolling his eyes at Cassie.

Seth smiled again and walked to the back of the bus with Jonah.

"He totally likes you!" Cassie said.

Finally, Etoile didn't argue. She just smiled a bit dreamily.

Cassie looked out the window at The Gamut as they drove toward the gates and out onto the main road. The lovely trees seemed to fly past her, blurring into a perfect shade of green. So much had happened in just a few days and she had the urge to text Erin back in Texas. It had been almost four whole days since they'd been able to talk! Cassie dug through her backpack and found her phone. She turned it on and was delighted to see that there was a text waiting for her from Erin.

CMP GRL! MISS U! HOW WAS IT??

Cassie quickly hit REPLY but she didn't even know how to put it into words. She thought for a moment, looking out the window again. And then it hit her. There was no way to explain this adventure in a text. She wanted to spend the time looking out the window at beautiful, splendid nature.

Of course, she would call Erin the moment she got home to tell her everything that had happened.

But until then, Cassie sat back and gazed out the window at the beauty of Maine, surrounded by her friends.

check out

Life, Starring Me!

another

candy apple book . . .

just for you.

"*Bon anniversaire, ma chérie,*" Great-aunt Silva said, leaning over to give me a kiss on each cheek. "That's French for happy birthday, my dear."

"I know," I said, even though I didn't. Pretty much the only French I knew was *oui* (yes), *non* (no), and *un croissant chocolat, s'il vous plaît* (a chocolate croissant, please). I guess some people might have learned more French after living in Paris for six weeks . . . but those people weren't starring in the international touring company of *Bye Bye Birdie*. I was.

Okay, it's not like the neon lights above the theater read BYE BYE BIRDIE starring RUBY DAY! But I had a very crucial part. A featured role. I played Randolph, the main character's little brother.

Yes, I was playing a boy.

So what? Like Great-aunt Silva says, vanity has no place in the theater. Even though I loved my long, thick, chestnut-colored hair, even though I'd been growing it out since I was seven years old, I knew the show was more important. So I cut it all off before the audition.

I got the part.

It wasn't my first big break. When I was six, I starred in my local theater's production of *Annie*. Then it was *Les Miserables*, at a big theater in Los Angeles, and after that, two national tours: *Mary Poppins* and *Gypsy*. I got *Bye Bye Birdie* when I was eleven, my first international tour. We hit Beijing, Barcelona, Buenos Aires — and those were just the B's. I'd visited almost fifteen countries — and I hadn't been home for more than a week at a time in two years.

That's where Great-aunt Silva comes in. My mom and dad had to stay back home in California with my little sister, Alana, so Great-aunt Silva came on the road with me. She homeschooled me in hotel rooms all over the world. She taught me how to say "yes" and "no" in thirteen languages. And most important, every day, no matter what, she got me to the theater on time.

"Through rain, sleet, flu, or yawn," she always says, "whatever it is, the show must go on."

And she should know.

Great-aunt Silva was an actress herself, forever ago. No, not just an actress — a diva. A *star*. She performed on Broadway until she got tired of staying in one place. ("I got too big for Broadway," she always says. "Or maybe Broadway got too small for me!") Great-aunt Silva never had any kids, either. She says she wanted to fly free, like a bird without a nest.

"I simply cannot abide the little brats," she huffs, every time we get bumped off the sidewalk by a horde of kids coming home from school. "But you're different. Do you know why?"

I'm always ready with the answer she wants to hear. "Because I'm a star."

Then she laughs. "Not yet," she reminds me. "But we're working on it."

Great-aunt Silva hates the movies. "They're nothing but smoke and mirrors," she says. "A pale imitation of life. The stage *is* life."

And okay, in some ways, she's right. The stage is *my* life.

But when it comes to telling a good story — like, say, the story of me — sometimes movies can come in handy. If this were a movie, here's where I would stick the opening credits. (So make sure you picture my name coming first, in huge, hot-pink letters that fill up the whole screen.) Over the credits, I'd show a jumble of scenes of my six weeks in Paris, all mashed up together. Because that's what it feels like to be on tour — you're never sure what day it is or what time it is or sometimes even what country you're in. We'd been performing in Paris for six weeks, and in some ways, it felt like six minutes. In other ways, it felt like a lifetime.

So take a bunch of mixed and muddled memories, add some slo-mo, a spiffy song, and — don't forget — my name in lights, and you've got your opening credits montage:

Scene: There's me, Ruby Day, and the cast of *Bye Bye Birdie* performing a special concert in the giant cathedral of Notre Dame. An audience of almost 5,000. Our music echoing against stone ceilings that stretch up a hundred feet over our heads. Dappled light filtering through a 700-year-old stained-glass window.

Scene: A grand ball at the Louvre, Paris's most famous art museum, in honor of some famous French guy. Fancy dresses and fancier appetizers. The *Mona Lisa* hanging on the wall, giving us all her strange half smile like she's got some particularly juicy secret. A special performance of songs from *Les Miserables*, featuring me, Ruby Day, singing my all-time favorite, "On My Own." (And singing it in French, which is harder than it looks. Trust me.)

Scene: International singing star (in training) Ruby Day, besieged by fans outside the theater's stage door. Signing program after program for a gaggle of shy, giggling girls. People see the crowd and get curious. "You someone famous?" they ask. I always shake my head no, but if Great-aunt Silva gets to them first, she tells them I'm a Swedish rock star or exiled Bulgarian royalty or the latest winner of *America's Next Hot Top Pop Star*. And when they get all excited and ask for my autograph, too, I put on a fake accent and sign a name for them. (*A* name, not my name. Often Penelope Pomplemousse, but sometimes I go with Stella Artichokie.)

Scene: "Lovely night for a moonlight picnic, Mademoiselle Pomplemousse," Great-aunt Silva says as she hops the low fence and clambers aboard the houseboat.

"You sure about this, Great-aunt Hildegard?" I ask, still standing on the edge of the Seine, looking doubtfully at the boat. Yes, it's the middle of the night and there's no one in sight. Yes, there's a picnic table and two chairs on the long, flat deck, perfect for eating *croissants chocolat* under the moonlight.

No, the boat doesn't belong to us.

"*Bien sur,* Penelope," Great-aunt Silva says, and she dangles the bag of croissants, knowing I can't resist.

I hop the fence.

Scene: The greatest night of not just my life, but *anyone's* life. Backstage passes to a special, private concert given by Patti LuPone, the greatest living Broadway diva. And not just backstage passes, not just a private audience with Patti LuPone herself, not just a handshake from the greatest living Broadway diva, but a *gift*.

Well, not really a gift — more like a sweaty old scarf that she was about to throw in the trash before Great-aunt Silva rescued it for me.

"That's kind of awesome," I say. "And kind of gross. It's totally soggy with sweat."

She looks at me like I'm nuts. "It's the sweat of a *genius*," she points out. Still, we carry it home in a plastic bag. Which works great until the wind blows the bag out of her hand, through the air . . . and into the river.

"The scarf!" I shriek.

Great-aunt Silva doesn't panic. She looks at me. She looks at the scarf, floating down the river. With a small shrug, she kicks off her shoes.

Then, even though it's December, she jumps in the river.

When they pull her out, looking like a drowned French sewer rat, she's shivering almost as hard as she's laughing — and she has the scarf wrapped around her left fist.

"Are you insane?" I hug her, even though now we both smell like dirty Seine water.

"It's *Patti LuPone*," she says, like I'm the crazy one because I didn't jump in. "What else was I supposed to do?"

End Scene.

Even a movie can only give you the highlights — the biggest, best, brightest moments. It glosses over all the little stuff in between, like the fresh crepes filled with hot, gooey Nutella; the window-shopping along the Boulevard Saint-Germain; trying on ridiculous feather-covered dresses no one could ever afford. (And who would want to?) Not to mention the room service, the cast parties, the hours and hours of rehearsing, the performances, the standing ovations, and did I mention the autograph signing?

Okay, I know I mentioned the autograph signing, but I figured I'd mention it again because it was awesome.

Some things sound like they'd be really fun and exciting and glamorous, but when you actually do them, you find out they're about as exciting as a field trip to a wax factory.

But starring in the international touring production of *Bye Bye Birdie* wasn't as good as it sounds.

It was better.

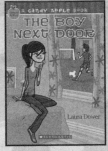

Read them all!

Accidentally
Fabulous

Accidentally
Famous

Accidentally
Fooled

How to Be a Girly Girl
in Just Ten Days

Miss Popularity

Making Waves

Totally Crushed

Callie for President